Ijiraq

Journeys of the Immortal
Book Two

Joel Thomas Feldman

First edition: February 2022

Cover art by Casey Gerber
Edited by Author Connections, LLC
Book Design by Crystal MM Burton

ISBN: 978-1-7353546-2-0
LCCN: 2021922263

Published in the United States by Joel Thomas Feldman
Please direct all correspondence to joelthomasfeldman@gmail.com
www.joelthomasfeldman.com

Dedicated to:

Indigenous peoples around the world

FORWARD

Welcome to the world of the Tahltan Nations, and the mythology of the Ijiraq. This is the second book in the *Journeys of the Immortal* series. As with all fantasy stories, reality is often suspended to express the fanciful tales you've grown to know and love. This book is no different, though a brief introduction is necessary to set the stage for the adventure that waits for you in these pages.

To start, you should know that the Ijiraq are not a part of Tahltan beliefs, but rather the Inuit. I wove the Ijiraq myth into the Tahltan world based on the characters and how I wanted the story to evolve. There is little information on Ijiraq mythology, and much of what you will read is my own mythology of the creature, which builds upon the sparse information I could find.

The Tahltan are a First Nations people who call northern British Columbia home. Their community encompasses 93,500 square kilometers and centers on three main population centers: Dease Lake, Telegraph Creek, and Iskut. Ijiraq takes place in and around Telegraph Creek, which sits on the Stikine River, a once-popular stop for prospectors on their way to the Yukon gold rush region. The place names herein are actual locales.

The Tahltan language, known as Na-Dene, is traditionally oral (passed down through dialogue, story, and dance). A written system of the language has only recently been developed. I used the Tahltan language in this story sparingly (primarily for character names). In that light, it's essential to understand that some liberties were taken for the sake of the story. For example, the word 'Dene' means 'People', and 'Dene Ti'e' means 'Boss'. To simplify, and because I could not find an appropriate Tahltan replacement, I shortened the term for Boss to the more straightforward Dene, and used it to mean Chief. The glossary at the back of this book defines the few words I've used with links for you to explore more about the Tahltan language.

That brings me to the word I just described: Chief. It should be duly noted that many indigenous peoples throughout North America no longer use this terminology, but the Tahltan do, according to their governance website (www.tahltan.ca/band-council), though they also use the term, President. By tradition, the Tahltan are a matriarchal society, where women hold the primary positions in government and leadership. As such, Ijiraq holds to that matriarchal order of power. However, creative license has been taken in describing certain characters as 'princesses' or 'queens'. This does not hold true in modern Tahltan society, but for the purposes of this story, it was used to establish relationships of importance to the overall arc of the series.

Finally, I would like to discuss indigenous beliefs. What

some may think of as mythology or mysticism, is anything but for indigenous people. The stories, laws about creation, folklores, and legends are a way of life. They are lessons on how to live and take care of the land, and each other. Indigenous people talk of spiritual gifts, not 'magical powers,' as is often seen in the fantasy genre. Where traditional literary terms and phrases are used which, without context, could be considered offensive to the Tahltan and indigenous peoples throughout the world, I want to make it clear that in no way does this book intend to make light of any cultural or spiritual beliefs.

If you are interested in learning more about the Tahltan and other First Nations peoples, please refer to the links below:

www.tahltan.ca

www.tahltan.org

www.firstnations.org

www.rcaanc-cirnac.gc.ca

I'd like to extend special thanks and recognition to two First Nation members who have guided me and helped me to understand their culture: author Elaine Alec, and former three-term President of the Tahltan Nation, Annita McPhee.

I sincerely hope you enjoy the journey on which you are about to embark.

—Joel Thomas Feldman

3

PROLOGUE

Raven: A Tahltan Creation Story

R aven was a benevolent but wily creature. He could transform into anything that suited his needs.

Raven observed that the entire world and its peoples lived in darkness save for one man, his wife, and his daughter. They had daylight, the sun, and the moon, all of which Raven desired. So he devised a plan. He would turn himself into a speck of dust so small that he could hide in the daughter's food, hoping to be swallowed. She would ingest him and give birth to him, allowing him to also have daylight, the sun, and the moon. But the girl noticed the tiny speck in her food and told her mother, who promptly removed it.

Raven decided to try again, placing himself on the rim of the daughter's cup in hopes of being swallowed. This time she did not notice as she guzzled her drink and Raven with it.

In a few months, the girl's belly grew, and she and her

parents were curious about how this could be. After all, no one came around them, too afraid because they were the only ones with light. The day approached when the girl was to give birth, and the mother told the father to build a small brush house in which to live until after the baby was born. This was their way—that the man should not live in the home until after the child was born.

The day of his delivery came and passed, and the boy grew quickly. His grandparents were overjoyed and doted on the child. Before he could speak, the young boy pointed to the skies—to the daylight—desiring to have it. The grandparents were wary, but they did not want to disappoint their grandson or give him reason to cry, so they handed him the daylight, which caused him great joy.

They relished in his exuberance, though it was short-lived. The boy wanted more—he wanted the sun, so the grandfather pulled the sun from the sky and handed it to the boy, who played with both of his gifts. Sadly, the boy was still not satisfied; he cried and cried in hopes of acquiring the moon. His grandparents did their best to give him other things to play with, but to no avail, and ultimately, they appeased the boy and handed him the moon so he would stop crying.

Now in possession of all three—the daylight, the sun, and the moon—the child wondered if he could fly through the tiny chimney of their brush house with his new baubles, but as much as he tried, he could not. He tried and tried,

5

never giving up until one day he was strong enough to hold the three objects and escape through the smokestack.

When daylight broke, all of the world's animals settled where they were, and that's where you will find them to this day. The bear in his den. The beaver in his watery dam. The birds in the trees. Raven brought them daylight, the sun, and the moon—as the world has been ever since.

CHAPTER ONE

Heads snapped to investigate the source of the racket as the rusty Bronco squealed to a stop. Throngs of teenagers, with their usual short attention spans, didn't break their gaze on the old jalopy. They recognized the vehicle and knew who was about to emerge. It was the first day of school, and most, if not all of the student body, had been waiting for this moment.

"Do I have to, Dad?" Sam whined. "Look at them. They all think I'm a freak show."

"Just take a deep breath and be confident. This is the first day of high school for a lot of people, not just you. I have no doubt you'll make friends fast."

"But Dad . . . "

"Have a great day, Princess. I'll pick you up after school. I love you."

Sam grudgingly exited the car, most eyes still fixated in anticipation of her grand entrance into the public spotlight. She slammed the door behind her as her dad

reiterated his gush of affection. It went unreturned.

Sam lowered her head and allowed her hair to help her avoid eye contact as she hurried her way across campus toward the school's main doors. She could hear the whispers, and worse yet, her classmates' unspoken thoughts flooded her mind—a cacophony of honest questions and musings mixed with disdain—those who thought her too different for their liking. Sam beelined it for the bathroom in hopes of a quiet respite. She'd stay there until the bell rang, with her headphones firmly implanted and music loud enough to drown out everything but the kerrang that would officially begin her high school experience.

Hovering above the toilet seat, Sam's face contorted in disgust. Mold filled the cracks of the pale blue tiles behind the commode; the stench was nearly unbearable. Thankfully, the bathroom door blocked anyone from having to endure her grimace. Dark, heavy electronic dance music exploded through her headphones—anyone who walked in might think there was a rave in the bathroom, complete with smoke from the upper-class girls who used school as their place to rebel. Experimenting with cigarettes was the least of it.

Sam pulled the schedule from her backpack. First period: Biology. *First period.* Thank God it wasn't three weeks earlier. Sam was a late bloomer, or so Mick told her. Newly fourteen years old, the stress of losing her mother, being hunted by a sociopath, and saving Ash had all taken a

toll. Her relatively new supernatural abilities and her name on the lips of everyone in Sedona only added to the feeling that her life was spinning. When she saw that her cycle had started, Sam had been ashamed and confused. *What was her body doing? Why?* Her dad had never talked to her about this, never warned her or prepared her. Perhaps he never thought to, or maybe he was too embarrassed.

Sam was grateful that Mick was there to help her navigate the introduction into womanhood. It should have been her mom, but even three years later, the sting of that giant loss had not subsided. Significant life events would always be bittersweet.

Before she was ready to leave the safety of the stall, that dreaded sound blasted through the speaker above her head and Sam was shuffling to class, the voices of her peers once again invading her thoughts. On any typical day, Sam could tune it out—a feat that had taken over a year to accomplish, with daily training and the help of her mentor, Mick. However, the anxiety of being in the spotlight didn't afford her the concentration necessary to find peace, and Mick couldn't chaperone her every time things got a little tough. The noise in her head was overwhelming, and before Sam could take a step into the classroom, she found herself exiting the rear of the main hallway, moving toward the wooded area past the athletic fields. Only then did the voices fade, allowing her to take a deep breath of relief.

"So, how was your first day, darlin'?" said a familiar

drawl from behind a tree, startling Sam.

"Mick? What are you doing here?"

"I could ask you the same thing, but I already know the answer. I take it things didn't go as planned in there?"

"Planned? Maybe not having a plan was my problem. I could hear everything, Mick. They were all laughing at me . . . gawking. I'm a sideshow."

Mick grabbed Sam and squeezed tight. Sam allowed herself to go limp, accepting the embrace. Mick was the first and only female role model in Sam's life since her mother's passing. It wasn't the same, but on a day like today, beggars couldn't be choosers. Sam needed motherly love, even if not from her own flesh and blood.

"You gonna tell Dad?"

"I think you know me better than that. I'm no rat. But you can bet the school will do that for me. Don't worry about your pops right now. Let's get your head straight. Bell Rock?" Mick suggested.

Sam shrugged her off. "Devil's Bridge."

Mick let out a belly laugh. Sam enjoyed the tone immensely; it made her smile every time. "Feeling a bit punchy, huh?"

Sam nodded.

"Alright then, Devil's Bridge it is." Mick led Sam to her Jeep and they made their way toward the trail head, just north of town. Despite the name, there was nothing dangerous or sinister about the natural red rock arch. The trail was heavily traveled by hikers looking for that Insta-worthy picture, standing on top of the archway, tempting fate on a ledge only five feet wide and fifty feet high.

Sam, though, preferred the view from below. It was there that she had discovered a very weak vortex earlier that summer. It had become her favorite spot.

Sam had discovered her sensitivities to the Sedona vortexes rather quickly: fields of swirling energy had caused her debilitating vertigo. Even the trees were not immune, many twisting in the most beautiful, unnatural ways. When her dad moved them there to escape the pain of Seattle, they had never heard of these vortexes. It didn't take Jack long to realize that every time they drove past Bell Rock, the airport, or any of the numerous sites in and around Sedona, his daughter winced in pain, and in a few instances, Sam had passed out.

Thankfully, Ash had flown into her life at just the right time. The phoenix showed her that not only did she have powers, but she could control the energy of the vortexes to her benefit—her weakness had become her strength. Despite Mick's own supernatural abilities, she could only guide Sam so far. Sam was far more powerful, like nothing anyone in Sedona had encountered. It's why she stood out at school and why icy glares followed her in public. She still wasn't

used to the stares and whispers, catching the thoughts of passersby, which she could hear in her head.

After Ash returned to his own realm, Mick had taken it upon herself to mentor Sam. It wasn't long before the girl was eavesdropping on everyone's thoughts, healing minor wounds by laying her hands on them; and even creating swirling, blue balls of energy in her hands—a party trick that she'd yet to find a use for, though she suspected it could lay quite a wallop on an unsuspecting attacker.

Pulling her powers from weak energy fields had become Sam's drug, proving to herself just how powerful she was becoming and that she no longer needed an intense vortex like Bell Rock. Sam's ability to manipulate the larger vortexes had become child's play. It was the small pockets of energy, like Devil's Bridge, that piqued her interest now. It took immense concentration to pull trickles of energy from her surroundings, imperceptible to the average person, even Mick. Sam basked in the challenge.

Seeking new ways to exercise her gifts was the one thing that made her genuinely happy and gave her peace. Most times, she played the role of a moody, disembodied teenager, having endured more than her share of tragedy in her fourteen short years.

As they pulled up to park, Sam's stomach turned.

"Looks like someone beat us here," Mick said.

"You said you wouldn't . . . "

"No blame here. That school of yours must be awful

quick with the truancy calls. It's okay; just take your medicine, and hopefully, your dad will be understanding. He usually is."

Before she could exit the vehicle, Jack made his way over and helped Sam out, shooting Mick a disapproving glare in the process. "Care to explain?" he demanded.

"I'm sorry. The voices were too much, and everyone was staring," Sam pleaded.

"And what's your excuse?" Jack said to Mick.

"No excuses here. I had a hunch this might happen. I was just trying to be supportive."

Jack turned to Sam, "Go get in the car. I'll be right there." He waited for Sam to close the door before laying into Mick, but Mick jumped in before Jack could say something he'd regret. "You do realize she can still hear everything you say, right?" It was rhetorical, but it still needed to be said, more to shut Jack up than to protect Sam.

It worked; Jack relented.

"Listen, Jack, go easy on her. Put yourself in her shoes. Everyone's talking about her, and kids can be cruel. We need to be there for her, even if it means she misses some school. She's a smart cookie, probably smarter than most of her teachers. Maybe there's another way. Homeschooling? I'd be more than happy to tutor her, although I suspect she'd be the one tutoring me most of the time." Mick chuckled.

From a distance, Sam's voice echoed from the rolled-down window of the Bronco. "Please, Dad?"

Jack turned and smirked, a raised eyebrow instructing his daughter to roll the window back up and be patient. Sam complied. "Let me think about it, Mick. Homeschooling a teenager—much less a kid like Sam—is an awful lot to take on. Are you sure you're up to it?"

Mick nodded, and Sam's screams of excitement from the car were audible, even with the windows up.

"I said I'd think about it."

"She's growing up fast. Maybe having her at home will be good for both of you. She needs her dad . . . I'm not telling you how to live your life, Jack, but you have a lot you still need to discuss with her."

"I know. It's just never seemed like the right time."

"It never will be. Don't make her wait much longer. It isn't fair to her, or you."

Jack knew what he had to do. He had been putting it off for too long. Nan had made him promise not to tell Sam until she was sixteen, but after seeing her courage and the adversity she faced with Ash, Jack thought she could handle it. He had doubled back on the promise to tell Sam several times already, using his wife's dying plea as an excuse to keep the secret, but Mick was right. It was time.

Sam was still listening to every word from afar, but Mick had learned to use her powers to keep Sam from getting in her head. She used every ounce of energy to ensure Sam wasn't preying on her dad's hidden thoughts as well.

"You're right, again. You're always right," relented Jack, and he bid her adieu.

Sam knew her dad had been keeping something from her—something that rightfully belonged to her—but she chose to pick her battles, focusing instead on convincing her dad to let her be homeschooled. She attempted to speak, to start litigating her case for never returning to that awful school, but Jack lifted a finger to his lips, preferring a quiet drive home. There would be plenty of time to argue her case soon enough.

The following day, Sam arose to a clatter. The sounds were foreign enough that she wasn't quite sure what to make of it. She tracked the rustling to her dad's room and knocked on the half-open door.

"Dad? Everything okay?" Sam noticed the half-packed suitcase on the bed. Jack was in the walk-in closet, buried to his shins in a heap of clothes. Sam walked in as he extricated a sizeable down coat from a box above his head. "Going somewhere . . . cold?" It was a two-part question.

"Oh, hi dear. Did I wake you?" He handed her the fluffy garment so he could keep the box above from falling on his head.

"Expecting a snowstorm?" Sam sensed her dad's diligence, but attempted to break his focus.

"No, not exactly. Well, maybe. It's hard to say."

"How long will you be gone? I take it Mick will be watching me?"

"We will be gone for as long as it takes."

Sam could see the vision in his head. Snow, ice-covered roads, wilderness . . . darkness. "A Bigfoot lead?"

Jack stopped what he was doing and sat her on the bed. "You and I are going to British Columbia."

Sam's excitement got the better of her. "Yeti hunting??"

Jack laughed at her exuberance but corrected her assumption, knowing the real news was even better. "No, Princess. I think it's time to take you to meet your mom's side of the family—the Tahltan tribe in the far northern part of the province. You have a lot to learn about where you came from. Your mom wanted me to wait until you were sixteen. We were going to go up there as a family, but I think it's time. You're old enough and mature enough to appreciate your ancestry."

"Really? I get to meet cousins and uncles and . . . "

"And your grandmother."

Sam never knew she even had a grandmother on that side of the family. Her mother never talked story about her relatives, and she had been too young to realize things were being kept from her. Even at the funeral, not one person from Nan's side came to pay their respects.

Jack blamed himself. It wasn't that they disliked him— Nan's family hadn't attended their wedding, either—they wanted Nan to marry within the tribe and carry on their traditions.

"My grandmother?" Sparks started to jump from Sam's fingertips. Her blue eyes glazed over—opaque sapphires. For the first time in a long while, she was ecstatic.

Jack grinned wide, pleased with her reaction. She could have been annoyed, angry even, that this knowledge had been kept from her, her whole life. He could foresee that was still coming once she had time to process. "Go get packed. Warm clothes!" He shouted but the girl was already back in her room, throwing clothes from her dresser onto her bed. It was the end of summer and the weather would be turning soon, especially that far north.

Sam snapped from her trance-like focus on her clothes. "What about school?" she yelled down the hall. She didn't really care about school but played it up for her dad.

Jack appeared in her doorway. "We'll learn along the way. Perhaps work on some geography: Utah, Idaho, Oregon, Washington."

"Seattle!"

"Especially Seattle." Sam jumped into her dad's arms. They had not been back to the Pacific Northwest since they moved to Arizona. Sam knew it would come at a price—the painful memories of her mother throughout the Emerald City. But she also knew they'd get to see Charlie and the boys.

Most importantly, Tommy.

CHAPTER TWO

A re we there yet?"

The drive north from Arizona was a long one. Sam, the impatient teenager, was showing herself early—it had only been eight hours into the twenty-plus hour trip.

The fourteen-hundred-mile trek to the Pacific Northwest was mostly unremarkable from what Sam could remember; nothing but desert and lots of farmland, endless rolling hills. She had been too young to appreciate the beauty of America the last time they'd taken this journey. Aside from well-known sites like the Grand Canyon, she hadn't thought to pay much attention.

Jack glanced at his daughter, not willing to entertain her whining.

Sam knew there was a long way to go yet, but she couldn't help giving Jack a wee bit of grief, despite the impending excitement. She couldn't wait to get to Seattle and see Tommy. Little did she know there would be a detour

ahead which would take them a few hundred miles—and hours—out of the way, but through some of the most beautiful mountain vistas of northern Idaho. Jack would wait to say anything, for now.

Sam feigned disappointment and donned her oversized headphones, quickly getting lost in thought. The drone of repetitive bass beating from her music forced Jack to push the volume on the car radio higher, to drown out the sound. *Kids' music these days.* He immediately recognized the irony as his own high school memories flooded in: long hair, black clothing, heavy metal and his parents' insistence that it was the devil's music and would make Elvis roll in his grave.

As miles of unimpressive scenery rolled by, Sam closed her eyes with thoughts only of Tommy. It had been over eighteen months since she had seen him, but not a day had gone by in which they didn't text or call one another. Sam wished they could talk now, but the dead zone they had been driving through prevented it, and her thoughts soon turned to her mom. She was trying her hardest to avoid the memories, but to no avail. Sam needed Tommy today more than most. It was the anniversary of Nan's death. Jack had not mentioned it once, and she was unsure if he even remembered.

Sam's wish was granted as her phone lit up with a text.

Tommy: *U ok?*

Sam: *I just miss her so much. Can't believe it's already been 3 yrs. Dad's acting like it's just another day.*

Tommy: *Give him a break. He hurts every bit as much as u do. I'm sure he's dealing with it in his own way. Have u tried talking to him?*

Sam: *Not yet. Until yesterday, he was still preoccupied with Ash. He rarely even sits down to dinner anymore.*

Sam meagerly looked up to ensure her dad wasn't paying more attention to her typing than the road. Jack smiled at her, solidifying her skepticism—he was oblivious of the date.

"You doing okay, Princess?"

Sam couldn't hear him with the music blaring, but the message came through loud and clear. She pulled a speaker off of her left ear and mumbled. "Yeah, Dad. Fine." She repositioned the headphone and turned up the volume louder still, now fuming inside at her dad's indifference. She returned to Tommy.

Sam: *He's clueless. Driving down the road with a dumba$$ smirk on his face as if nothing is wrong.*

Tommy: *I'm sorry. But I still think u should talk to him.*

Sam: *Ok, fine. I'll try. I've forced myself into his head a few times, but he doesn't like it when I do that. TTYL. Love u.*

Tommy: *Love u 2 . . . Princess*

Sam responded with an eye-rolling emoji. Jack's nickname for her had never really bothered her, but she wasn't okay with anyone else using it, even in jest . . . even Tommy. She knew he was only trying to get her to smile, but it annoyed her.

"Dad?" Sam removed her earmuffs and lowered the car radio. "When are you are planning on telling me whatever it is you need to tell me?" She was calm at the moment, but anxious, and hoped she could keep her temper in check.

"What are you talking about, Princess?"

"Come on, Dad. I know you've been keeping something from me. I've tried to figure it out, but Mick keeps blocking me . . . and she isn't here now."

Jack attempted to think about their detour instead, hoping it would distract her.

"Wait, where are we going?"

Jack's thoughts had turned to the idyllic mountain town in Idaho where they were headed. Sam could see the images—and the vision of a brand new vehicle with a sticker still in the window. "A new truck?!"

His tactics were working.

"I was waiting to surprise you, but I guess I can't keep you out of my head. Yes, a new truck. There's no way this old beast is going to survive the harsh conditions up north."

Sam was happily surprised, but thoughts of new car smell and comfortable seats only distracted her momentarily. "Awesome, Dad. But you still haven't answered my question."

Jack dropped his shoulders and knew he couldn't keep it from her any longer. "I really wanted to wait until we get there, but I suppose now will do. Your mom wanted me to wait until you were sixteen, but I think you're ready." Jack quickly got lost in thoughts of Nan and her passing. "I suppose today would be more appropriate than most."

Sam was relieved; he hadn't forgotten. She lightly touched his shoulder, in hopes of imparting some peace—he was struggling.

Jack appreciated the gesture. It confirmed her maturity and readiness for the news.

Sam decided to stay out of her dad's head and receive

the news naturally. "Thanks for trusting me," she said. "I'm sure Mom would have been okay with it."

Jack pulled to the side of the open highway. The sun was setting, and despite needing to eat and rest for the night, they were still fifty miles from their evening layover. He couldn't wait and wanted no distractions—he was uncertain how Sam would react to the revelation.

Sam was jumpy, trying her best to concentrate on anything other than the thoughts going through her father's head. Jack slowly reached into the interior left pocket of his jacket, to fetch the bauble that would open up a whole new world for Sam. Her eyes widened in anticipation of the item securely tucked into Jack's palm, save for a few links of the chain which glimmered in the waning light. Sam extended a trembling hand, and he deposited the gift safely where it would always stay.

Dangling from a delicate gold necklace was a heart-shaped locket made of what appeared to be intricately carved granite. The artifact was familiar, and Sam's eyes instantly flooded—it was the same heart that had adorned the boulder, and later, the cave that led her to Ash. The same heart which glowed when touched and caused the winds to howl and the waterfall to become suspended, and without which she never could have saved him.

"It was Mom?" Sam said in disbelief. "But . . . how?" Questions were racing through her mind so fast that she couldn't formulate a straight thought.

23

"It was Mom."

"Why didn't you say anything?"

"At first, I wasn't convinced; it was all a little too coincidental. But after the heart at the cave appeared, I started to believe. I wanted to tell you, but I didn't want to go against her wishes. I probably should have told you after everything with Ash, but I was afraid. Please forgive me."

Sam wanted to be angry, but the sorrow was overwhelming, despite a hint of joy. The wound was reopened—Nan died once again, and all Sam could do was yearn for her mother's embrace.

Jack searched for words of comfort, but could see the hurt he'd inflicted and couldn't bear to do any more damage. The remainder of the news would have to wait. He placed a comforting hand on the back of Sam's head. He wanted to hug her, tell her it would all be okay, but . . .

The locket, tucked into Sam's palm, began to glow. A brilliant blue light pushed through the cracks and crevices, illuminating the carved swirls as if trying to cleave the amulet. Just as fast, the light faded. Sam frantically examined the locket, looking for a seam that might open the rocky exterior, but no clasp or hinge was present.

"Let me see, Princess."

Jack did his best to pry the locket in half. He grabbed his pocketknife, but before he could do any potential damage, Sam stopped him. This was a gift from her mother. As much as she wanted to see what—if anything—was

inside, she had no intention of damaging the precious heart in that pursuit. She retook possession of the locket and placed it over her head, tucking the heart into her shirt.

"That's never happened before, I swear." Jack hurried to explain before she could get mad. "I tried once several years ago to open it, but never could."

Sam's pain and sorrow were gone. "It's okay, Dad. I think that was Mom trying to talk to us, to let us know she's okay and not hurting anymore." Sam was indeed at peace, possibly for the first time since Nan passed. Even after everything with Ash, she had never shown this calm. "Let's go, I'm hungry."

Jack pulled the car back onto the highway, relieved by Sam's newfound peace, though somewhat dismayed by her belief that Nan was back with them—alive.

Her spirit was present and now hanging adjacent to Sam's heart.

With darkness fully set in on the desolate road, Sam stared up at the moonless heavens. The stars were as bright as she had ever seen them, the Milky Way painting a swath of white through the night sky, almost enough to light up the surrounding mountains. Her thoughts were on her mother, and Sam unknowingly clutched at the locket through her shirt. She knew that if she could see inside the heart, something magical awaited.

Sam's concentration was broken by the buzz of her phone—Tommy checking in, making sure they had arrived safely for the night. Sam was never one to not respond to him almost immediately, but she wasn't ready to tell him her news quite yet either.

Sam: *Almost there. TTYL.*

Tommy responded, clearly in a talkative mood, but she brushed him off. She had too much on her mind, and though he had become her safe space, her comfort, and often her strength, right now Sam was content meandering through memories of her mom.

Without warning, the tires squealed, and crunching metal gave way to a solid object propelled into the windshield, nearly into the cab. Sam slammed forward, the seatbelt keeping her from smashing her head against the dashboard. Jack wasn't as lucky; blood poured from a cut just above his left eye due to his glasses being pushed into his face. Then the sounds faded, replaced with eerie silence.

Sam looked through the shattered glass to see a large deer carcass splayed across the hood. Its antlers had pierced the windshield directly between them—a foot in either direction, and the results would have been unthinkable. Life was draining fast from the creature's large dark eyes.

"Are you okay?" Jack asked.

"Yeah, but you aren't. You're bleeding pretty bad."

Jack reached for his forehead and winced when his fingers found the wound. "That thing came out of nowhere." The deer twitched, clearly not yet gone. Sam couldn't stand to see the beautiful animal in so much pain.

"We need to do something, Dad."

Jack unbuckled and exited the mangled vehicle and headed to his toolbox in the back, which had opened, spilling most of its contents. He found what he needed and made his way toward the deer.

"Dad! No!" Despite a lack of light, the gleam across the edge of the large blade caught Sam's eye. "Don't, please!" Sam fought with her seatbelt, still pleading with Jack not to kill it.

"Sam, it's in pain. It's best this way. This was just an unfortunate accident."

Sam finally freed herself of the restraint and rushed to place herself between her dad and the animal. "No, it's not the best way . . . or the only way."

Sam turned her back to Jack, closed her eyes, and began to concentrate. Reaching out with both hands, she laid them on the bloodied hindquarters of the deer, which flinched, causing Sam to react in kind. Slowly, she replaced her hands and the animal remained calm. Its pain resonated through her, but she pushed through and reassured it that she was trying to help.

A soft white glow began to emanate from Sam's hands

and envelop the deer. She didn't budge, concentrating as hard as she could, but nothing happened.

"Sam," Jack said. She didn't let it break her focus. "Sam, it's gone."

She started to relent, pulling her hands back when a warmth began to emerge from under her shirt. Before she could look to see what was happening, the blue light from the locket had returned. Without hesitation, Sam redoubled her efforts, sharpening her concentration. The corpse was again wrapped in white light, now joined by the blue light from the heart. Jack had to shield his eyes from the brilliance.

The glow finally dissipated into the cold, late summer night air. They watched as the deer began to twitch. Life returned to its eyes, and its head slowly lilted from side to side, attempting to remove its antlers from the windshield. The creature was eerily calm as it tried freeing itself, and once it had, it pranced toward the tree line from where it had first leapt. Before it disappeared, it stopped and looked back toward them.

"So, that's a new one," Jack said in amazement. "Learn that from Ash?"

"I must have. I've never done that before—not like that. I wasn't sure I could. I just had to try. Mom . . . "

"She helped." Jack finished, and Sam nodded.

"Come here, Dad." Jack stepped closer, and Sam placed a hand over the cut on his head. The white glow was warm, and Jack could feel the energy, the magic.

Sam removed her hand and immediately hugged him. Jack embraced her with one arm, using his free hand to verify the results. *It's gone.*

CHAPTER THREE

The morning couldn't come fast enough; neither Jack nor Sam could sleep that night. They had lost their appetite as well, given the carnage they endured.

The sky glow was barely visible, but they set out for the day, hungry and tired, and still a half-day's drive to the car lot. Sam's healing powers could do nothing for the nearly destroyed Bronco, but it remained drivable . . . barely.

Sam texted Tommy to let him know they were back on the road. The immediate response was unexpected. Tommy, being an hour behind, should have been asleep, or so Sam figured.

Tommy: *So early?*

Sam: *Getting a jump on the day and going to pick up the new truck. Go back to sleep. Zzzzz.*

Tommy: *Can't sleep. Feel like ur mad at me.*

Sam: *Not mad at u. Talk later. In person.*

Sam wanted to spill everything to Tommy, but she knew he'd only worry if he knew about the accident, and she wasn't ready to answer the barrage of questions about the locket or her newfound life-giving powers. She questioned how much she trusted him. Sam knew deep down she could, but the magic of the heart and her abilities . . . they scared her.

There was no way Tommy would feel any different about her because of it. He was always supportive, always there for her, and could always fix things with just a few well-spoken words. Still, she thought it best to wait until they were together, and out of sight and earshot of her dad. She needed to let him know how much she still cared.

Sam: *TY for always being there for me. I LOVE YOU!*

That should do it—ALL CAPS—to get the point across.

The remainder of the drive through the mountains of Montana and Idaho was silent. Occasionally, Jack would query Sam about eating or request that she turn down her music a bit, but otherwise, not a word was said. More than ever, Jack wanted to tell Sam about her mom, that she also had powers, that she was an actual princess. But he was still afraid of Sam's reaction, making her mad and losing the trust that took so long to earn after Nan's death. If it weren't for Ash, he might never have.

That new car smell filled Sam's head. Her mood lightened now that they were riding in style and a mere five hours from a Tommy reunion. The obsidian, heavy-duty truck was a beast, roaring down the highway with ease but still far quieter than the old Bronco they had just parted with after so many years: Sam could hear Jack clearly as they made small talk about the sights and sounds of Seattle, reminiscing about the time they had last seen Charlie and the boys . . . and Ash.

Jack saw his opening but was anxious, wringing his hands on the wheel while summoning the nerve to tell Sam the next part in Nan's story—in her story. He wanted Sam to know before they got to Seattle and was running out of time. He knew Seattle would become much clearer for Sam; memories would start to make sense.

"Princess? So, yesterday, when I gave you your mom's locket . . . well, there's more I need to tell you. I wanted to, but after everything—with it glowing and then the accident—it didn't feel right to dump more on you just then."

Sam stiffened in her seat, not sure what to expect next, bracing for the worst. The gift from her mom was a blessing, but she was fearful and worried about whatever knowledge

she was about to receive.

Jack continued, "Your mom was special . . . like you. She had abilities."

Sam was floored. "Wait, what? Mom had powers? Like what?" Sam could not believe what she was hearing. It all made sense now; they had to come from somewhere. She had assumed it was Ash who bestowed her with these supernatural gifts. After all, she could harness the earth's natural energy, invoke fire from thin air, and now heal the mortally wounded. Had she absorbed Ash's abilities? But perhaps it was her mom, not Ash, who provided her these powers.

"Your mom could control the elements. Earth, water, fire . . . "

"Air," Sam said, confirming what she already suspected: it was Nan who had created the wind funnels and stopped the flow of the waterfall.

"And the other elements as well."

"Other elements? I thought there are only four?"

"Actually, there are eight, but most people are only familiar with the big four. There's also light, darkness, ice, and nature (basically, plants and animals). Your mom could control them all."

"But why wouldn't she want me to know? Why didn't she show me herself?"

"She did, when you were much younger, before you knew any different. Do you remember those rainy days where you 'got lucky' and didn't get wet running to and from the car? Or the small waves that carried you back to shore when you were learning to swim? Or the oddly strong breeze that picked up all the leaves in the yard, which you danced around in?"

They were early memories for Sam, but it all started to make sense. The young child hadn't known to question what was happening. It was natural and not the least bit unusual. "I don't understand. Why did she stop? How old was I?"

"You were five and just about to start school. Your mom didn't want you to be singled out and ridiculed by the other kids. She was afraid for you. All she wanted was for you to have a normal childhood, but she knew that her powers—and yours—could make you both a target for bullies and non-believers. I never saw her use her powers again. I promised her I'd wait to tell you. She wanted to be sure you were mature enough to handle the responsibility."

"I've always had powers? That means I could have saved Mom!" Sam said, her response bordering on anger, believing her mom could still be alive if they had allowed her to use her healing hands.

"No, Princess. We talked about that, but you had no training, and the little bit of magic you did possess would not have been enough. Even if your mom had trained you, the amount of energy required . . . you wouldn't have been powerful enough."

Sam turned sullen, tears rolling down her pale cheeks. She wished they had given her the chance to save her mother, even if a long shot.

"To be honest, we never knew you possessed the ability to heal. You used to make small whirlpools in the bathtub, but we didn't know the scope of your abilities beyond that. Your mom could tell that you were very powerful. What happened yesterday was incredible, and she would have been just as surprised; it's not something she could do. Her mom—your grandmother—is a healer for the tribe, but your mom was never taught to use those abilities. Your grandmother didn't want to burden her with every sick or dying person she came in contact with. I suppose there's a strong lineage of protecting future generations from undue stresses related to your powers."

Sam wiped away her tears. She had so many questions about who she was and where she came from, but would keep them to herself, for now. She wanted answers, but her head was swooning with so many conflicting thoughts. She was ready to see Tommy and tell him everything, to be in his arms, knowing he would say just the right thing to calm her down.

A few hours later, Sam got her wish, arms wrapped tightly around Tommy's neck. She had forgotten how he felt, how he smelled. There was a sudden realization that she was on her tiptoes, with her neck craned, and staring into those dreamy eyes—*he's so much taller!*

"Well, hello to you too, Miss Owsian," Tommy said with a chuckle.

Sam released her vise grip, "Hi there, Mr. Stevens."

"What are we, chopped liver?" It was Chris, Tommy's older brother. He was more handsome than she remembered, a man now. He had turned eighteen a few weeks earlier.

Sam and Jack made the rounds, greeting Chris, Eli, and Charlie with hugs and taking in how much the boys had changed. Eli was almost as old as she was when they discovered Ash, though he was hardly recognizable. Long gone was the chubby-faced little kid who was constantly stuffing his face, always hungry. "Wow, Eli! You look great!" Jack said. "Very fit. Been working out?"

"Thanks, Mr. Owsian. Carbs are the enemy, ya know. Dad, what's for dinner?"

"As you can see, not much has changed around here," said Charlie.

Except for the bear hug she laid on Tommy, Sam gave Charlie the biggest hug of all. He had put them through hell, lost complete control, and nearly killed them. But if not for Charlie, they never could have saved Ash and protected his immortality.

It had taken a long time for Jack to forgive his old friend. In the heat of the moment, Jack had pushed aside his

distrust and anger, caused by Charlie's reckless behavior on that trip. It wasn't until Jack had time to contemplate his friend's inexplicable acts that raw emotions surfaced. The college chums, both adventure seekers, did not speak for six months after the incident. It had taken Sam to show Jack that Charlie was still the good person he'd always known.

"Come, let me show you what I've been working on," Charlie said excitedly. He had just returned from a trip to the Arctic Circle, investigating recently unclassified Russian intelligence reports of an extraterrestrial ship, which military witnesses claim crashed into the polar ice caps in the 1960s. Jack would have customarily accompanied him on such an expedition, but had declined in favor of his own work: trying to piece together the existence of mythological creatures beyond Ash. His decades-long search for Bigfoot had taken a backseat in favor of his personal, tangible experience with a real-life phoenix.

Sam and Tommy slipped out the back door, not keen on another fanciful lecture about aliens, or the ensuing debate their dads would surely devolve into. Fingers interlocked, they strolled the greenbelt along the Seattle waterfront facing Puget Sound. The weather was temperate, the sun was shining, and Sam couldn't be happier, fully present in the moment with her beau.

"I missed you," she said.

"I missed you, too." Tommy waited for her to continue, but she was silent. "Is everything okay?"

Sam smiled and pulled him behind a tree, out of view from other pedestrians using the walkway, and kissed him—their first kiss since that moment of excitement on Bell Rock celebrating the rebirth of Ash and Cinder. The kiss was longer and deeper than anything they had shared before, but was interrupted when Tommy let his hands slide down Sam's backside, which she was quick to swat away. Things had changed. They were growing up fast, and the puppy love they shared nearly two years before was blossoming into something more adult—something Sam was not quite ready for, though Tommy seemed to be. She wouldn't compromise her virtue, even for him.

"Hands to yourself, please." Tommy mumbled a meager apology, his cheeks turning crimson at his unsuccessful, brazen attempt. Sam knew how sensitive he could be and grabbed his hand again, reassuring him. "I love you, Tommy. Not yet, though."

Sam had lost sense of who she was with the news of her mom's powers, and it was a perfect opportunity to cool Tommy's jets and tell him everything she had learned on the drive northwest. As they continued down the greenbelt hand-in-hand, Sam let loose about everything that had happened, most of which was recounted through tears. Tommy had a hundred questions, but knew better than to interrupt. When she stopped talking, he turned toward her and placed a comforting hand on her cheek. "I love you, Sam." He would save his questions for another time. At this moment, his only job was to be there for her.

Most men two to three times Tommy's age still hadn't figured out when to shut up and just be present. For Tommy, it was innate. He was tuned in and really got her, and Sam loved him for it.

They returned to the house just as Charlie was finishing his heroic tale about braving the Arctic tundra and nearly losing three fingers to frostbite. He threw in a bit about how he incredulously escaped a charging polar bear defending her cub, but no one was biting at that fish tale.

Jack said, "Hi, Princess. We were just discussing . . ."

"Oh, I already know, Dad. I could overhear his whopper as we were walking up," Sam said with a lighthearted laugh.

"It's all true, Sam. I swear," replied Charlie, who made no attempt to hide his crossed fingers. "So I hear you have quite a story yourself, missy. Healing powers? Like Ash? Like Nan?"

"Not like Mom, but yes. She had other powers."

"So I've heard. I guess royalty has its privileges, huh, Princess?" Sam was confused by the remark. Only her dad—and occasionally Tommy—called her by that name. Never Charlie, not even in jest. He continued, "Who would have thought your grandmom was an honest to goodness chief?"

"Charlie," said Jack, waving him off and shaking his head. But it was too late; Sam had heard what she heard—

everyone heard—and a conflicting sense of anger, clarity, and confusion reverberated through her. She was reading her dad's thoughts and could see the truth, the rest of the truth he had yet to tell her. Sam didn't say a word. She simply waited for an explanation.

"She didn't know? Oh, Jack, I'm sorry. I thought you told her." Charlie blushed from his lack of candor.

"She knows now, Chuck. Thanks for that." Jack's tongue was sharp, and rightfully so. The 'Chuck' jab was a less than flattering moniker Charlie had earned in college, but always effective in grabbing his attention. It let him know Jack was less than pleased with his slip up.

"I'm an actual Princess." It was a statement more than a question. The anger was welling, apparent by the sparks jumping from Sam's fingertips and the blue haze washing over her eyes. At the risk of his safety, Tommy grabbed her hand and squeezed in an attempt to calm her. It wasn't until he spun her toward him that her fire subsided.

"Can we discuss this later, honey? In private?" Jack pleaded.

"Honey? What happened to 'Princess'?" She was livid, and Tommy was the only thing keeping her from exploding.

Jack continued his pleas, but Tommy pulled Sam back outside to cool off. "Wow, so that happened."

"Of all the things to keep from me! Who am I?!" It was a genuine question.

Of all the revelations on this trip, this one caused her

the most pain, disconnecting her from everything she knew to be true about herself. She looked up at Tommy, but before he could provide his usual words of wisdom, she kissed him—mostly to shut him up.

"I know, I know. Talk to him. Listen to him. Give him a chance, yadda, yadda." Sam rolled her eyes, but Tommy embraced the attitude, knowing she had calmed, if only a little.

He tempted fate to ensure he was right. "You read my mind, Princess."

Sam glared at him, and then kissed him again. It was a welcome distraction from her doubts. She didn't want the moment to end, knowing that in the morning they'd be back on the road. She would have to face the conversation with her dad—one she hoped would provide answers and help her regain some sense of identity.

CHAPTER FOUR

T he eastern light broke the horizon and bathed the usually green Olympic Mountains in shades of oranges and reds. The sunrise created a fiery reflection on the calm water fronting the coastal peaks. Sam and Tommy had stayed up all night, not wanting to waste a moment of their waning time before they parted, and without a clue of how long it might be until they would see each other again.

Tommy wrapped the blanket tighter around them as they sat in silence, watching the current flow past them, a pod of orcas cresting the surface as they swam by. Sam continued to track the whales' path. She reminisced on a whale-watching trip she had taken with her parents—when her mom was still healthy, before any indication of the hell they'd soon endure. Jack had taught her how to spot the massive creatures by tracking glassy lanes of seawater on the surface, showing where the whales had been. It was also the day she learned that killer whales weren't whales at all,

but dolphins. She loved that fact.

"Can you imagine being free like that? Gliding through the water? Splashing, jumping, playing? No cares in the world?" Sam said.

"I suppose that would be pretty incredible . . . except for the eating fish and seals part," Tommy joked. "But a pod stays together as a family; they protect each other."

"I wish we could stay together." Sam tightened her grip on Tommy, not wanting the moment to end. She knew that any minute, her dad would call her name and their difficult goodbyes would commence.

"We'll still be together, just not physically. You'll have to protect yourself . . . though I don't think you'll have a problem with that. Me, on the other hand, well, I suppose I need to stay out of trouble while you're gone."

"You better!"

Tommy knew exactly what she meant—other girls. She knew she didn't have to worry about him; he was faithful and would never do anything to hurt her. But she didn't trust the unknown—the throngs of girls at school who undoubtedly had an eye on him. He was even more handsome now that he'd grown out of that awkward tween phase. Tommy was tall and lean, with a dashing smile and incredible eyes. Sam always found herself getting lost in those soft brown peepers, and she could only imagine other girls did too. She took solace in the fact that Tommy didn't know how attractive he really was. He remained hidden in

Chris' shadow during his first two years of high school. But with Chris graduating, Tommy had become more noticeable among his classmates—only he hadn't realized it. Sam was perfectly okay with that.

"I love you, too," Tommy said, kissing her on the forehead.

The new truck barreled down the highway with ease. It had been three hours since Sam was forced to drive away from Tommy, but the tears had not stopped. Jack wondered if it was excessive, but quickly squashed that thought, knowing if it were Nan, he'd be the same way. He still found himself inconsolable at times, especially when it would hit him that he'd never get to see her, hold her, or kiss her again. Jack wouldn't force Sam to deal with her sorrow any way other than her own. If she wanted to talk, he'd listen. If she wanted to be alone, he'd give her space. He decided to settle into the drive, not expecting any conversation any time soon. He still needed to explain more about her royal background and her mom's side of the family, but he'd wait until she was ready.

"I'm ready, Dad."

Of course, you were listening, Jack thought.

"Sorry," was all Sam could get out through her sniffles.

"I can only tell you what your mom told me. She wasn't too keen on talking about her past. I'm hoping your grandmother can fill in the gaps once we get there."

"If I'm a princess, and mom was a princess, then is Grandma a queen?"

"Yes and no. Your grandmother and grandfather were both considered royalty—he was also a Tahltan Chief, but from a different clan. Your grandfather's clan was represented by the wolf, and your grandmother's by the raven. It was their union that brought the tribe together under one rule. Before that, they were one people, but lived apart except to trade and barter. They did band together at times, though, to fend off settlers looking to exploit the area's natural resources."

"I thought you said you didn't know much, Dad?"

"Well, I did some research, so it's not all from your mom." Jack continued to explain how the society was matrilineal, and despite her grandfather having been Chief, he was more of a figurehead than true royalty. Her grandmother was the rightful ruler of her people, though she never considered herself a queen.

"Matrilineal? Meaning that everything is passed down through the women?" Sam knew she was right but wanted to hear her dad say it.

"Exactly, Princess." Hearing Jack call her Princess had a new connotation; it actually meant something and wasn't just a pet name. Sam's hesitance at the moniker had grown old as of late, but now it created a sense of pride not there before.

"There's one more thing you should probably know before we get there." Sam braced herself for another life-changing revelation about who she was. "Your mom's tribe never accepted me. They blame me for her never returning home after college. She didn't go back to take her place and lead her people as heir to the tribe. And . . . "—tears welled in Jack's eyes and his voice began to tremble— "they blame me for her death. It's why no one came to the funeral. Even our wedding was only my family. Your mom never cared, or at least she never showed me that she did. All she wanted was our family; we were all she needed to be happy."

Sam's already-wet cheeks felt fresh tears fall as she listened to her dad's heartbreaking story. She couldn't imagine the pain, had Tommy's family not accepted her or if they had treated her like an outcast. "What's going to happen when we get there?" Sam was worried for Jack's safety if they were so unabashedly hateful of the damage he'd caused to their tribal legacy.

"I'm counting on your grandmother to be the voice of reason. She's the one person who never showed me anything but love. All she wanted was for your mom to be happy, and if that meant marrying outside the clans and never returning home, she was okay with it."

"Then why didn't she come to the funeral? Why have I never met her?"

"It's not an easy trek for someone her age. And my guess is no one was willing to help her."

"Can't she just order them? If she's in charge, then . . . "

"I've only met your grandmother once, but she didn't strike me as someone who rules with an iron fist. She's compassionate and empathetic . . . like your mom."

"I thought Mom never went back?"

"Not to stay. Before you were born, when Mom was pregnant with you, she took me up there in hopes of changing their minds about me. She hoped that if they could see her happy and healthy with a new tribe member on the way, they'd lower their guard. But only your grandmother shared in our joy."

"I'm sorry, Dad. But don't worry, if anyone tries to cause trouble, they'll have to deal with me." Sam rolled a ball of blue fire in her palm, passed it back and forth between her hands, and gave Jack an all-too-sinister smile.

"I think we'll be okay, Princess, but thank you."

The remainder of that day's drive was jovial. Father and daughter reminisced about Nan and eventually got to talking about Ash, and how much they wished she could have met the magical bird. Sam missed Ash tremendously. Despite their short time together, those three days defined who she had become. She had found an inner strength she never knew existed.

The following morning, Sam roused from a deep sleep. Her head had hit the pillow while waiting on their motel room pizza delivery the night before. Jack was still snoring, and the half-eaten cold pizza called to her. She was famished. The long road and heavy emotional toll of the last few days had been taxing.

Sam checked her phone, but there wasn't a single message from Tommy. Disappointed but not despondent, she pinged him. Soon enough, they'd be back on the road and undoubtedly out of cell coverage. Tommy's response was immediate, but the conversation was short. Sam knew something was off, but she convinced herself it was all in her head, despite the nagging concern. She hoped when they arrived at their next stop she'd be able to video chat with him—or at least call him—and read his thoughts to ensure it was nothing.

Another eight hours on an endless two-lane highway. Sam was weary but attempted to distract herself with the scenery—lush, hunter mountains, crystal lakes, and the abundant wildlife that thrived in this remote area. A bald eagle the size of a reborn Ash flew alongside them for

nearly a mile. Sam occasionally checked her phone, but service was spotty at best, and even when she had a bar or two, no messages came through.

They pulled into the blink-you-missed-it town of New Hazelton, still a full day's drive from their final destination. The tiny hamlet was quaint but rather plain, the only remarkable feature the ominous mountain, casting its shadow from above. Sam was in awe of its surreal beauty. Snow blanketed the upper half of the sheer peak, and conjured visions of dragons and medieval creatures.

As Jack checked them into their next home away from home, Sam rustled through a pamphlet she chose from a dusty rack near the front desk. Hagwilet Peak, also known as Stekyoden or Stegyawden, climbed 2076 meters above the New Hazelton skyline. Whatever the name, it belonged at the center of an epic fairytale, where knights and wizards battled ogres and their hellhounds, defending the citizens fortressed inside the ice castle built into the summit. The people would celebrate the eventual victory and their continued freedom from the invaders with a grand feast and masquerade gala inside a crystal ballroom.

"Sam!" Jack said in a raised voice. She snapped out of her daydream, mildly peeved, not realizing he had been attempting to get her attention for some time. "Ready to go?"

Sam grabbed a few more fliers to peruse in the room. There was no way she'd find anything to watch on television in this podunk place—she wasn't convinced there would even be a TV.

The room was musty, and the drawn curtains allowed only a sliver of light that revealed a beam full of dust motes. Sure enough, there was a television, though it looked like something out of the 70s—or what Sam assumed a TV from then looked like. Jack could read her face and couldn't help but chuckle. "You'll live, Princess. It's only for one night."

She checked her phone to see if she at least had a signal. To her surprise, a few messages were waiting for her, including a photo of Tommy that made her stomach turn. He was as handsome as ever with that heart-melting smile. Being without him, dreading the unknown, wondering what he was doing and who he might be talking to—made Sam feel sick. She shot back a reply, including a cute picture of her own, but it went undelivered, which made her cringe. His phone was either off or dead.

Sam needed a distraction and picked up the stack of handbills advertising everything from skiing and back-country hiking expeditions to helicopter tours and horseback riding. "Dad, can we do something?" She waved the flier for a chopper tour of the surrounding mountains.

"I'm not so sure about a helicopter tour; it sounds a little dangerous. Besides, it's a little late in the day for that. We should probably get something to eat and rest. Chinese?" Jack waved his own paper, a menu from the nightstand drawer, but received only eye-rolls.

50

Sam was restless and made one last feeble attempt. "What about this?" She handed Jack a pamphlet for a short hike to New Hazelton Waterfall: 'a small but picturesque, three-tiered cascade over moss-covered trees and rocks amid a dense aspen and hemlock forest.' With barely an hour of daylight left, Jack hesitantly grabbed the truck keys and motioned for Sam to get her coat.

The trailhead was a mere five blocks from the motel, but they drove nonetheless. The hike in was only a quarter-mile, but the setting sun and thick foliage made for a darker, more difficult path than they'd hoped. A frigid breeze cut through the trees, but Sam knew better than to complain. This was what *she* wanted, after all, in her begging pleas for a cure to her boredom and loneliness.

As they reached the falls, the sights and sounds hadn't been done justice by the brochure. The sun was sinking just below the top of the highest chute, pushing through the trees and creating rainbows in the fine mist. Even Jack couldn't help himself from pulling out his phone and snapping pictures. It didn't escape Sam's notice. As long as he didn't start taking selfies like a teenager, she'd keep quiet and let him enjoy the view.

"Thanks, Dad. I really needed this."

"No, Princess, thank you. I guess I didn't realize I

needed it too. I should probably listen to you more often." Sam tilted her head and shrugged in agreement.

After a few more minutes soaking in the wondrous vista, the sun had fully dipped behind the waterfall, leaving them in darkness. Despite the well-worn path, it was difficult to see. They were thankful it was only a short walk.

Sam removed the phone from her pocket to light the trail with the flashlight, but before she could turn it on, a movement in the corner of her eye caught her attention. She turned but saw only the faint outline of trees and bushes. Sam squinted, but nothing appeared. Then another image moved in the same direction as the first, but she saw something this time: horns.

"What is it, Sam? What's wrong?"

She lifted her hand to silence her dad while still trying to track the movement, but it had stopped. "I'm not sure. A deer, I think. It was just odd that as soon as I turned to face it, it seemed to disappear. I could only make out the faint sensation of something in my peripheral vision; like it's watching us but doesn't want us to see it."

"Probably just a skittish animal. I'm sure you're right; this place must be crawling in deer. Probably moose, too. Maybe we should hurry back; they're known to be quite aggressive."

As they refocused on the path, Sam once again caught a glimpse of the elusive animal. She fought the urge to look in the direction of the creature, instead using her side-eye—

perfected over time when unhappy with her dad. She spotted it. The horns were tall—easily half its height—and it appeared to have red eyes that glowed in the waning light. It was standing . . . upright.

"Run!" Sam yelled. Jack didn't hesitate and was right on her heels. They didn't stop until they reached the truck, attempting to catch their breath.

"What did you see back there?"

"Its eyes were glowing, and it stood on its hind legs, like a human, but it had massive horns like an elk." Sam was shaking uncontrollably. "Dad, I could hear its thoughts. It warned us to leave. To go away and never return."

Jack helped Sam into the truck, and they hurried back to the safety of their room.

Immediately, Jack pulled out his laptop and started scouring the Internet. What he found frightened him, too. He read, "Wendigo. A mythological creature or evil spirit of Native American origin, known to possess humans and resort to cannibalism. They are often depicted as up to fifteen feet tall, gaunt, and possessing horns."

"They eat people?!?" Sam replied in horror.

"Yeah, I just lost my appetite, too. We need to leave first thing in the morning and get as far from here as possible."

"Back home?" Sam hoped.

"We've come this far; I think we should keep going. The tribe should be able to protect us and perhaps tell us

53

more. If the Tahltan live among these things, I'm sure they'll know something."

They would wait until full daylight to leave, not willing to take a chance on exposing themselves again at night. Jack and Sam were restless and hardly slept, worrying the beast would hunt them down and make an example of them for others who failed to heed its warnings. The television stayed on all night, as well as the lights. Darkness was not their friend this evening.

CHAPTER FIVE

The highway to northern British Columbia was long and winding, mountainous, and dangerous if the late summer weather gave way to an early winter wonderland. The weather, though, was the furthest thing from their minds as they trudged toward their final destination.

Wendigo.

Evil spirits.

Possession.

Cannibalism—Sam cringed every time she thought about it.

Two years earlier, the possibility of such a thing would have been decisively dismissed, even despite Jack's belief in the supernatural, his wife's abilities, and his life-long hunt for Bigfoot. But Ash, and Sam's newfound belief in the arcane, changed everything—it upended their world and everything they knew to be real.

Not wanting him to worry, Sam said nothing to

Tommy about the incident with the Wendigo. Knowing they would have inconsistent cell coverage the rest of the trip, even once they arrived at Telegraph Creek, she kept the conversation light and joking. Sam hated keeping anything from him, and guilt over the ease which she did made her uncomfortable. She would tell him, just not now.

"Last stop, Princess," said Jack as they pulled into Dease Lake. The town was a central Tahltan community; Jack hoped no one there would recognize him. "We just need to gas up really quick. Looks like a front is moving in, so we need to hurry. You want to go in and grab some snacks or something to drink?"

Sam was excited to get back on the road and meet her family, and the further they got from New Hazelton, the less frightened she became. However, going into a gas station convenience store brought back unpleasant memories of watching her dad get hauled off to jail for stealing Mick's Jeep. "I'm good. I just want to get there."

The route from Dease Lake to Telegraph Creek was a windy gravel, road that followed the Stikine River through a steep, narrow valley. The water was murky from upstream churn caused by late summer rains. Springtime and snowmelt would eventually transform the river into a crystalline pathway through the emerald expanse.

Only sixty-seven miles separated Sam from her destiny, but Mother Nature would test her patience. Within minutes of leaving the gas station, snow started to fall.

Gently at first, but the deeper they drove into the valley, the heavier it came down.

"Snow in the summer. Wow," said Sam in awe.

Jack grew more nervous with each passing mile, creeping through the growing drifts that covered the road. The lanes were no longer visible, and a drop-off on the right side of the highway plunged down to the river. Jack slowed further, but as he lightly pumped the brakes, all four wheels broke free and they began to skid sideways. Sam screamed. Jack counter-steered in hopes of keeping them from going over the edge, but they continued to slide. The truck turned away from the ravine and came to a halt only inches from the opposite embankment.

"Are you okay?" Jack asked. Sam nodded, wiping hair from her face. "I'm not sure if we should keep going; it's getting worse by the minute. I think maybe we should wait it out or hope someone comes along who can help."

Sam rejected his options and offered her own. She brought her hands together in front of her face—palm to palm, as if praying—and a ball of light formed, engulfing her hands. She propelled the blue-green light through the windshield toward the road. The snow in front of the vehicle began to melt, revealing the wet gravel beneath.

"I plow, you drive?" Sam asked with a mischievous smirk.

"Think you can keep that up for a while?" Jack asked. Sam's beaming confidence was all he needed.

Jack continued at a crawl, despite a quark of cautious confidence thanks to Sam, and two hours later, they arrived. It was just as Jack remembered: a few simple structures weathered by harsh winters, save for the large, modern-looking tribal hall; rows of nondescript homes perched on the river's edge; and an old church, whose spire rose higher than any other building in the village—a landmark which could be seen from anywhere in town. At the center of the village was a wide-open space that held a short stage—the dais, on which a brass bell with a pull-string hung from a rusty fulcrum.

They proceeded slowly. The tribe had been expecting them, and many parka-covered faces lined the streets to unceremoniously welcome them. The stares were deep, the unspoken choir of distrust and questioning running through Sam's head.

They slowed to a halt at the end of the road where the tribal hall stood and were confronted by four stark faces. Two were younger. Sam presumed one to be around her age—a girl with dark, expressionless eyes. The boy was older, but he, too, remained stoic and cold. The closeness with which they stood to the man led Sam to believe this was their father. She immediately knew the last of their reception party. The old woman's face was new but familiar. Her eyes were tired, but still shone with the same radiance as her mother's.

"Grandma," Sam said as she exited the truck. She

didn't wait for her dad. Sam shuffled toward the old woman—much shorter than herself—and jumped into waiting arms. It was as though she were hugging her mother again. Grandma even had the faintest scent of cloves and allspice, intensifying memories of Nan. Waves of tears warmed Sam's cheeks. She couldn't let go. She didn't want to. She was home.

"Welcome home, dear Sam. Let's go inside and warm up."

Sam nodded, taking note of her grandmother's voice, the intonation and cadence with which she spoke—*just like mom.*

Jack accepted a forced smile from the man and followed in silence. The lack of acknowledgment was expected, but hurt nonetheless.

Once sheltered from the arctic weather, a roaring fire greeted them in the foyer of the hall. Large river-rounded boulders, stacked with precision, rose from floor to ceiling. The hearth was enormous, large enough for the stern-looking man and his children to stand upright inside its cavernous space if the fire were not present. A pine mantle jutted from over the opening, holding several Tahltan artifacts: a stuffed crow in mid-caw and a menacing wolf sat on opposite ends, protecting the treasures. It was the object front and center, though, that caught Sam's attention—she couldn't look away.

"Welcome, Jack. It's so great to see you," said the old

woman. The humph that followed from the man confirmed to Jack that despite his mother-in-law's greeting, he was unwelcome. The man was corrected without delay. "Enough, Daniel. You will treat our guests with respect. There is no place for anger here. The time for that has long passed."

Daniel turned away in protest, but did not dare question her.

"Thank you, Rose. It's wonderful to see you, as well." Jack was tentative, but accepted her reception with a returned hug. Like Sam, tears welled, as Rose was the closest thing he had to Nan outside of his daughter.

"Grandma Rose?" Sam said, still staring at the stunning yet frightening object on the mantle.

"Call me Nana. That is the name we use in these parts for us old folk." She chuckled at her own amusement. The boy and girl joined in, but Daniel remained stone-faced, wishing Jack gone with his icy glare.

That name pulled Sam from her trance, a reminder of her mom. Her mother was everywhere she looked. This had been her home.

"Nana, what is that?" she asked, pointing to the ominous centerpiece. A golden mask shimmered in the firelight. The resemblance was unmistakable—the long face and ruby eyes examining her, shadows and light coming to life in its hollow eyes. Atop its head, a magnificent crown of antlers, twisting and coiling, ready to impale anyone who dared cross its path. The beast. The Wendigo.

"That's a ghost story told to scare children, but very much a part of our ancient heritage and beliefs."

Daniel spoke. "It's real." His words were foreboding. There was fear in his eyes, as though he had encountered the creature. It was a warning. The girl smirked as her brother cowered. She enjoyed watching her dad bait their guests.

"Enough, Daniel. You're scaring the kids," Nana scolded.

"Who's scared?" the girl argued with a glance toward her brother.

Rose snapped back, "Show some respect, Maddie." With that, the girl fell silent and her face flushed. "Daniel, please show Jack to his quarters. Take Ted and Maddie with you to help with their things. Jack, if you don't mind, I'd like some time with Sam?"

"She's in great hands, Rose," Jack said.

Daniel and the kids escorted Jack back into the cold and toward the truck, where they started to unload suitcases. Not a word was said, and the tension made Jack anxious. They entered a building on the far side of the tribal hall, which Jack noticed was attached by a long, covered hallway, the walls of which were made of large glass panels, frosted over from the wintery conditions. Once inside, it was clear this was a dormitory of some sort. Jack had never been in the building on previous trips and wondered if it was designed to be a school, perhaps for visiting tribal kids staying in Telegraph Creek.

Daniel opened the door to one of the rooms and haphazardly dropped Jack's belongings on the floor. "Welcome home," he said sarcastically as he turned and walked away.

Ted and Maddie continued two doors down with Sam's items and set them in her room. The rooms were plain. Steel frame beds pushed against the exterior gray brick walls. A single window above let in a small draft, enough to chill the space and make it ever so slightly uncomfortable. Each room was furnished with a metal desk and chair and adorned with two small-framed black and white pictures. From what Jack could tell, they were photographs from the 1940s or 50s depicting an unknown tribal ceremony.

"Is there a restroom?" Jack called out, noticing that the accommodations more closely resembled a college dorm than a motel room. He didn't receive a response.

"So you want to know about that, huh?" Nana asked, and Sam nodded at the horned creature staring them down. "In due time, dear. First, I want to hear all about you."

Rose's joyful demeanor was infectious, but Sam was

still hesitant, not ready yet to talk about her mother. She felt strangely at home in this place, but shy and cautious at the same time.

"What do you want to know?" she asked her grandmother.

"Your dad says you had some adventure a few summers ago. I hear you've learned quite a bit about yourself and who you are."

"Yes, Nana." Sam didn't realize she was clutching her mother's pendant and tugging the necklace so tight, it was on the verge of snapping.

Nana stared long at Sam's hand, wrapped around the locket. "Why don't you show me?"

"Show you?" Sam was wary that her dad had said too much. The weight of the moment hit her hard and without warning. She opened her hand to reveal the heart-shaped object, now glowing softly. "If I have . . . and mom had . . . then you . . . ?"

Nana Rose snapped her fingers and a cherry red spark danced on her fingertip. She swirled her finger as the magic she commanded grew and created a scintillating tornado that reached to the ceiling and surrounded them, engulfing the massive hall room. Sam's mouth was agape at the power she was witnessing. "Now, you."

Sam joined her grandmother, creating that familiar teal glint and pushing it upward, twining with Nana's magic. Before they knew it, they were laughing hysterically, pushing

and pulling the choreographed dance of two minds, two magics, two generations separated by a missing piece, but still somehow whole and in sync. It was a joy Sam had not felt since her mother was alive. In training, she'd performed magic with Mick, but the connection she was feeling with her grandmother was something new, something special.

The performance continued until another voice was laughing with them, catching Sam off guard. She stopped, embarrassed by what someone else may have seen. It was Maddie. "It's okay, Sam. She knows. Although not all Tahltan have these abilities, she is one of us." Maddie approached, a soft green glow peaking from her closed palms. She opened her hands to reveal her own extraordinary power. "Sam, meet Maddie." The girls smiled easily at each other. The knowledge of each other's abilities created an instant connection.

"How long have you known?" Sam asked.

"As long as I can remember. Nana has been teaching me for years."

"Years? How old are you?"

"Thirteen next month. I hope you're still here. I would love for you to attend my coronation."

"Coronation? You're a princess?" Maddie and Nana nodded in unison.

Nana Rose said, "And so are you, my dear. But you already know that, right?"

Sam glowered, still not at peace with Charlie's slip-of-

the-tongue, and that her dad had kept it from her for so long.

Grandmother took notice. "Don't be angry. Your mother and father were doing what they thought whas best for you. But now that you know, I suppose a double coronation ceremony is in order?" Nana asked, expecting concurrence from both girls. Maddie's friendly demeanor turned in an instant; a pursed-lip smile a less than convincing response.

There was a hint of jealousy bordering on hatred in her eyes as she met Sam's sheepish gaze. Sam let out a nervous chuckle. A rivalry had been born, and Sam wanted no part of it.

"That's okay, Nana. It's Maddie's day; I don't want to intrude." Maddie gave Sam an accepting yet suspicious smile. It was too late. The friendship Sam had with her magical cousin had lasted only seconds. Maddie's contemptuous thoughts filled Sam's head.

"Nonsense, I insist. Maddie, please go let your dad know, so he may inform the council of our new plans." Maddie stormed off, but not before glaring one last time at her fellow princess.

"Don't worry about her, Sam. She's not as mature as you . . . or I." Rose chuckled, once again amusing herself.

Sam offered an awkward grin before returning her attention to the mantle and those haunting ruby eyes. They sparkled with an evil she'd never felt before.

"You can't stop thinking about it, can you?"

Sam averted her gaze from the beast, recounting her experience in the forest. The beautiful waterfalls juxtaposed by horrific images of the horned creature that had followed her in the corner of her eye. Recalling its warning to leave made her shudder.

Nana provided a calming touch, but not before correcting her granddaughter's identification of the monster.

"What you saw was no Wendigo. Although similar, the abomination you encountered is just as sinister. I have feared its return for a long time."

Sam shook in dread. "What is it?"

"The Ijiraq."

CHAPTER SIX

S am stared at the wall across the grand ballroom, which sat behind the foyer. The room was ornate and full of Tahltan artifacts, including a massive crystal chandelier that looked like it belonged in an urban art deco building, not here in the middle of nowhere.

The drab exteriors of the town's structures were countered by the beautifully detailed decor of the insides. Sam supposed that in a place where you had to endure nine months of winter with the majority of time spent indoors, it made sense. *Though, my room is certainly dull.*

The celebration to welcome her and Jack, and announce her as princess-in-waiting, along with Maddie, was a nuisance. The room was large enough to squeeze in most of the local tribe, and it felt like they must all be there. Sam was so focused on the far wall that the din of voices and clinking glasses and silverware that would usually (maddeningly) swirl through her head, was silent. Even the death stare and jealous thoughts from Maddie went

unnoticed. The Ijiraq mask and the story her grandmother just told her were all Sam could think about. She only wanted to find out more about the creature—*not a Wendigo*—that had warned her to stay away.

"The Ijiraq can only be seen by a shaman or those of us with special abilities," Nana Rose had explained. "They are shape-shifters, whose normal form resembles the caribou, but they stand on hind legs with eyes glowing red. Their mouths sit vertical, with rows of sharp teeth. They can take the shape of any creature they desire, but always with deep red eyes." The Ijiraq that warned Sam had revealed itself in its true, terrifying form, but the thought of the monster as a human, as Nana had described, was the stuff of nightmares.

"The Ijiraq typically appear as a fleeting movement from the corner of your eye. They can reveal themselves at will, but unless they do so, only those like us can see who they really are. Most see them as an animal, usually a raven. This is how they watch us, circling high above where the color of their eyes is imperceptible. The Tahltan revere the raven, so the presence of anything strange often goes unnoticed."

Despite the horrors of all she was told, it was what her grandmother said next that made Sam want to flee, to go home and never return.

"You must take care when you are alone. The Ijiraq can be helpful, but they are also quite deceptive. They can

disorient you and make you lose all sense of direction. It is in this way that they lure children away from their homes and steal them for their own use."

"What do you mean, 'own use'?"

"No one knows, dear. Only one child has ever returned after being abducted. It was as if her mind had been erased. She only remembers using the *inuksuk* to find her way back home. No recollection of what she went through or how she escaped."

"*Inuksuk?*"

Nana explained the stone formations, stacks of rock placed throughout the forest—landmarks, of sorts—to aid navigation through the woods and reorient those misdirected travelers who may be lost or led astray. Children learning tribal traditions are instructed to use *inuksuk* to find their way home if lost in the woods. It was a lesson taught early on, to those barely old enough to read, for safety and survival in the frozen, maze-like surroundings of the Stikine Valley. The name Ijiraq was never mentioned in regular conversation, but instead passed on through myths and legends—fairy tales, not reality.

"The truth is, the Ijiraq do exist, Sam, as you are well aware." Sam felt a chill down her back. "After the return of the lost girl, the Tahltan agreed to a truce with the Ijiraq peoples. They would no longer steal our precious children, and in return, we would provide a sacrifice once every eighty years, to maintain the peace."

"Sacrifice?" Sam knew where this was going, but needed to hear her grandmother say it.

"Every eighty years, we must hand over one of our own to the Ijiraq . . . "

Sam cut her off, not concerned about the rudeness or any perceived disrespect. "You sacrifice a child to them?! That's insane!"

"I understand how upsetting this is, dear, but please allow me to finish." Sam sulked back in her seat, hands glowing, but quietly listened on. "The sacrifice must be a child of consequence. One who possesses special abilities. Tribe royalty. One whose powers can sustain the Ijiraq for another eighty years. It is only in this way that we can maintain peace and avoid their terror.

"They have been restless lately." Nana paused, but knew she had to tell Sam. "Next week, in conjunction with the coronation, marks the eightieth year."

The wheels were turning at breakneck speed. *A human sacrifice? Royalty? Abilities?* Sam gulped at the realization. "Is that why I'm here?! I'm the sacrifice? A royal child with abilities?" Sam tried to process this sobering information. She felt a mild hysteria growing inside her. Not allowing her grandmother to break her thoughts, she had to ask. "Maddie was never an option, was she? I'm an outsider. Tahltan royalty, but someone the tribe would never miss. Just the long-lost daughter of a cast-out member of the tribe?!"

Sam's fear boiled away. Her anger spiked and she started to burn—an uncontrollable burst of energy from deep within, not just her hands and eyes, but her whole body so powerful that her usual blue magic turned white-hot. Even her eyes glazed over in a swirling, milky cloud. It knocked Rose to the floor and blinded her.

Sam snapped at the sight of her grandmother on the floor and the damage she had done to the room. The doors were blown open and a frigid wind poured in, adding to the chaos. Papers and books were strewn everywhere, and the artifacts from the mantle lay on the floor—the Ijiraq mask included. A section of the horns had broken off and settled at her feet, which she quickly kicked away.

Despite the horror of being the next Ijiraq sacrifice playing through her mind, she rushed to help her grandmother to her feet. Rose rubbed her eyes, willing them back into focus. "I'm sorry, Nana Rose," said Sam with lack of contrition. She was still angry, but thoughts of her mother calmed her and brought her back to a somewhat stable state of mind.

"You are powerful, like the raven, my dear. I never realize just how much so."

"I don't understand."

"The raven is our creator. Clever and strong. A hero, but prideful and stubborn, and, at times, uncontrollable in its selfish desires."

Sam's face reddened, her response sheepish, "I am

stubborn and selfish."

"You're missing the point, granddaughter. You are stronger than you know. You can create from nothing. You are just like your Nana and your mother. Perhaps stronger than the both of us combined." This was said with a mischievous smirk.

"Then why would you sacrifice me? Your own flesh and blood?"

"Sam, you will not be sacrificed. I would never allow it." She embraced the unsettled teen, hoping to impart some comfort.

"And Maddie?"

"She will also be safe from the Ijiraq."

"Then who?"

"We are unsure what to do at this point. As wise as I may seem, even I do not have all the answers."

"What will happen if you don't offer anyone up? Will they attack?"

"It's hard to say, but I imagine children will once again start to go missing. They are not a warring people, though an attack out of desperation wouldn't be out of line for them. They are secretive, choosing to live in between the land of the living and the dead. Scavengers, preying on the weak and unsuspecting. It's why a powerful royal is needed to satisfy their needs. One person can take the place of scores of non-magical children."

"It has to be me. I won't let your peace lapse." Suddenly,

Sam was no longer afraid. If what her grandmother said was true, she believed herself powerful enough to face the Ijiraq and survive.

"Sam, no. I will not allow it. I won't even discuss it."

"What happened the last time? Eighty years ago, someone was sacrificed then, right?"

"No one has ever been given up freely to the Ijiraq. This will be the first time the original agreement will be called to bear. I was just a little girl when peace was made between my father and the Ijiraq. It was I who escaped — the lone, abducted survivor."

"You?"

Nana nodded, "To this day, I still do not know what became of me after they took me. I was only four years old. I had been walking through the forest with my mother, picking berries and enjoying a hot summer day. There was a large bunch of fruit that mother couldn't reach without being pricked by the thorny branches. I wandered into a briar patch to fetch them for her and never came out. It's the last thing I remember until I walked back into the village several weeks later. My father surmised that my fledgling abilities and the *inuksuk* had saved me."

Sam's mouth hung wide, and a sudden realization hit her . . . *if Grandma Rose hadn't survived, I wouldn't exist.*

"Sam?" No response. "Sam!" Jack said, grabbing her shoulder to shake her from the daydream.

"Yeah, Dad. Sorry." Her concentration was broken; the flood of voices and thoughts returning to invade her mind. She winced, trying to force the rush of noise back out.

"Are you enjoying yourself, Princess?"

She stuttered, still trying to shake the recollection of Nana's story. "Uh, yeah, doing great." She forced a smile, but he knew better.

"Join me, Sam," he requested.

Jack took his daughter by the arm and escorted her into the tunnel at the back of the building. It wasn't heated, designed to be a pass-through only, not a loitering area or place to talk. Sam shivered, then released a soft blue heat that surrounded them and fogged the windows, blocking any prying eyes from outside.

Sam searched for movement or thoughts of someone or something that might be eavesdropping on them. She was relieved by the silence, but still feared seeing any fiery eyes or vertical smile that might penetrate the frosted windows.

Distracted from the conversation and whatever her dad was saying, Sam nodded and provided a string of robotic "yeah," "okay," and "sure" responses. She had

become a master of intermittent dialog with her dad and provided enough response to make him think she was listening. But Sam couldn't get the Ijiraq out of her mind, and what might happen if they did not receive their expected ransom. "Quid pro quo" was a phrase she'd heard often lately when watching the nightly news with her dad. *Is this the same thing?*

"Dad, I think I want to go to my room. I'm tired." She wasn't, not even in the slightest. She just needed to be alone in her thoughts and find a way to help her grandmother. "Please tell Nana Rose, I'm sorry. I hope she'll understand." Sam knew good and well that she would understand, but needed to play this game for her father's sake.

She returned to her room, but not before hiding around the corner to make sure Jack returned to the party. Once free, she gathered a backpack with some essentials, suited up in the warmest clothes she could find, and pulled on a pair of heavy-duty snow boots. It was time to head out.

It was pitch black, but Sam could make out the tree line to the north of town less than a quarter mile away. She would lay low, no lights, creeping in the shadows to avoid any attention. As she stepped into the forest, a rock formation caught her attention.

Inuksuk.

Two stacks, each four rocks high and bridged by a longer slender stone, sat at the base of the closest tree to the village. Sam examined the arch-like formation and wondered if there was meaning to how the stack was arranged. After all, these were used for navigation, so it seemed logical that different arrangements and heights of rock were meant to guide the user in a specific direction. Sam regretted not asking more about them, but it was hard to ignore the more significant revelations Nana had conveyed.

Attempting to stay unnoticed, Sam pulled a flashlight from her sack and adjusted it to its lowest setting. Her gloves were not holding up well to the now negative temperatures, so she allowed her hands to glow ever so slightly. It was barely visible through her mittens but visible nonetheless. It kept her warm.

Sam continued into the forest, careful to take note of landmarks and the direction of every turn. She was headed upriver but still insulated in the foliage, out of sight from the village. Within a mile, she had passed no fewer than six more *inuksuk* stacks, starting to see a pattern. Depending on how the rocks were positioned, they instructed to turn right, left, or continue straight. She purposely moved in the opposite direction, tracing the formations backward to see where they would lead.

After another hour, Sam found herself deep in the forest, out of sight and sound of the river. The night air temperature continued to drop, but it was clear since the

moon had risen big and bright enough to penetrate the treetops, allowing her to extinguish the flashlight.

A few more feet through a thigh-deep snowbank brought Sam to a large boulder. She hadn't seen any *inuksuk* in some time and was worried she had taken a wrong turn. *Did an Ijiraq disorient me? Force me to take a wrong turn?* She rested against the giant stone in hopes of gaining her bearings. The moon allowed her to make out the far valley ridge on the other side of the river. *Head toward the river, then follow it back.* She wanted to continue, but without the rock stacks to guide her way, she feared she'd get never make her way back before someone realized she was missing.

As she propped herself back off the rock, her finger grazed a large hole in the boulder. Even with her gloves on, she could feel the indention. Turning her flashlight back on to inspect, she saw something she never expected to see again—*the heart!* It was identical to the heart-shaped divots that led her to Ash in the Arizona wilderness. Identical to the heart that stopped the flow of the waterfall at the cave.

An unexpected warmth began to build on Sam's chest, and despite the layers of clothes, a light pushed its way through. She pulled the locket from the safety of her shirt, so bright that Sam had to shield her eyes for a moment.

She knew exactly what to do.

Removing a glove, she reached out and started tracing the outline of the divot. She got what she expected—it was glowing, just as blue and bright as it had back home. *Mom.*

The thought caused the heart to pulsate and grow even more brilliant—the pendant was in synch, matching the rhythmic beating. She was sure her mother was watching over her, keeping her safe in an unfamiliar place, guiding her.

She watched in awe as the heart-shaped trinket and boulder flashed and danced together.

Wait. Could it be?

Sam removed the necklace and held it closer to the divot. The beating increased, as did the intensity of the light. Sam fought through the blindness and pushed the locket into the hole in the boulder . . . *FLASH*. She was knocked backward but scurried to her feet immediately.

"No way," she muttered in disbelief. The necklace holding the locket had come to rest on top of the snow at the base of the rock, but the locket itself remained in its heart-shaped hovel—it was home. The light remained, though soft now, and calmly alternating red and blue. "Dad's not going to believe this."

The heart went dark as a branch snapped behind her, forcing her to take cover behind the boulder. The crunching snow under a heavy gait terrified her . . . she was about to come face-to-face with what she was looking for but never truly wanted to find. Sam peeked from her hiding spot and fell back into the cold embrace of the snowbank, a shadowy figure standing in front of her. She pulled her hands together and generated a fireball, propelling it toward her attacker, but she missed.

Sam scrambled to her feet and raced toward the river valley as fast as she could.

"Wait! Sam, wait!" said a new but familiar voice. She slowed, but kept moving away. "Sam, it's me. Stop, please!"

"Ted?" Sam reversed course and approached with caution. "What are you doing out here?" She wasn't happy she'd been followed.

"I saw you leave. I wanted to make sure you were safe. There's a lot of crazy in these woods that you're unaware of."

"So you stalked me for the last two hours? You're right; that is a lot of crazy."

"I'm sorry, I should have said something back at the first *inuksuk*, but I was curious what you were doing out here. I should have said something."

"Yes, you should have. It doesn't matter, though; I can take care of myself. And I'm fully aware of the Ijiraq. Nana Rose told me everything. Why do you think I'm out here?"

"You know, and still came out here by yourself . . . at night? What if they take you?"

"They won't. It's not time for the sacrifice yet. That's not for another week. I thought that maybe if I could find where they lived, I could help Nana figure a way out of . . . "

Ted interrupted. "Did you say sacrifice? Like a human sacrifice?"

"Why are you playing dumb? Yes, you know, the eighty-year sacrifice of a magical royal tribe member so your people can continue to live in peace?" The look on Ted's face

portrayed that this was not common knowledge amongst the tribe. He was genuinely mortified.

"Maddie!" He had put the pieces together rather quickly.

"Nana Rose can explain everything. I'm sorry, I assumed you knew. Can you get us back?" Ted nodded.

The walk back was relatively quiet. Ted tried asking more questions, wanting Sam's knowledge of the Ijiraq and the ensuing sacrifice he had to assume would be his sister. When Sam refused to comply with his query, he tried making small talk, but it was useless. Sam was a closed book, locked with a key he didn't possess.

All Sam wanted was to return to the rock and feel her mother's presence again—that and to keep Ted quiet about the information she let slip.

As they reentered Telegraph Creek, Sam finally spoke. "Please do not tell anyone we were out there. Understand? We'll talk to Nana in the morning."

"But . . ." Sam interrupted him with another swirling ball of light in her hands, and he fell silent.

"Goodnight, Ted."

Despite the threat, he liked the way his name sounded in her voice. Sam could hear his thoughts and scoffed.

"Goodnight, Sam."

CHAPTER SEVEN

Sam shook from a deep slumber, shivering and sweaty. She had been dreaming—more like a nightmare—of trying to escape from the red-eyed beast chasing her, but her legs wouldn't budge, stuck in cement-like snow and powerless to melt it with her abilities. The fear dissipated almost immediately with sounds of yelling and fighting outside. She checked her phone and couldn't believe she had slept so late: *11:00.*

Sam dressed quickly to investigate the turmoil, but could hear the cacophony in her head before she opened the door.

"Down with the Ijiraq!" yelled one man.

"Who sacrifices kids?" screamed another.

"You're killing our own people!" said a mother, clinging to her two young children.

Ted! Sam was furious that he had said something, that word was spreading before they could speak with Nana Rose.

Sam barreled outside, blinded by the intense sun

reflecting off the snowy ground. She rubbed her eyes, needing to find Ted and wring his neck, but instead was grabbed by the elbow by an unknown assailant and marched across the common. Sam's sight adjusted as she found herself on the dais.

The person manhandling her was none other than Daniel, a man she already knew was unhappy with their presence in Telegraph Creek. "Take her! She doesn't belong here anyway. You say she's a royal, and my daughter has seen her powers. So did Ted last night, when he followed her into the forest. She brought a boulder to life, making it pulsate with light, and unleashed an energy force that nearly knocked him to the ground. This girl is far more powerful than Maddie. She's worth more than eighty years of peace. She must be the sacrifice! We must renegotiate with the Ijiraq!"

Despite her meek and frail appearance, Rose had a booming voice that shushed most of the mob. "No one will be sacrificed. Do you understand me? No one, Daniel! Not Sam, and not Maddie."

"We thought the eighty-year sacrifice was just a story—tribal legend," asked another mother from the back of the crowd.

A timbre of hushed voices began to rise throughout the masses, and Rose raised her hands to quiet them. "I'm sorry, but yes, it is true. Council members had been sworn to secrecy, at risk of causing undue worry amongst you." The

82

concerned voices grew louder. "Please, be calm. We will figure this out, but rest assured, there will be no sacrifice of any kind. The Council will convene in an hour, and we will not rest until we have a solution. If you have constructive ideas, please write them down and drop them in the slot outside the Great Hall. We will provide an update on our progress this evening."

Rose and the rest of the council turned and retired to the tribal hall, ignoring additional questions, concerns, and anger.

Sam began to follow, but not before Jack got to her. "Sam, what is this all about? Why were you in the forest? And by yourself?"

"Apparently, I wasn't by myself." She had spotted Ted across the common, attempting to avoid eye contact with her. She forced a thought into his head: *You're dead!*

Ted turned toward the soundless voice and met Sam's menacing glare. Her hands glowed white-hot and his head dropped, like a dog with his tail between his legs, scurrying away.

Jack said, "Sam, focus. What is this all about? And no sass."

Sam told Jack of what she really saw near the waterfall in New Hazelton, what Rose had told her about the Ijiraq, and the truth behind the legend — the brokered peace which was up for renewal. She purposely left out her offer to Nana to sacrifice herself.

"So you thought . . . what? That you'd go hunt these creatures yourself? Then what?" Jack was beside himself at her brazen actions, her increasing powers making her reckless.

"I don't know, Dad. I just know I had to do something. Grandma says I'm far more powerful than her or Mom. I wanted to . . . "

"Wanted to what? Sacrifice yourself?"

Exactly. "It doesn't matter; I'm sure Nana will figure something out. And now that everyone is watching me like a hawk, I can't do anything anyway."

"They're not very trusting of outsiders. And as much as you are your mother's daughter, they still do not see you as one of them."

"Wait! Mom! I have to show you!" In the commotion, she had forgotten to mention the heart-shaped divot.

Jack was reticent to meet Sam's excitement, but hinted a smile she took as affirmation.

"Can we go? Like, now? Please? Pretty please?"

"Give me a few, Princess, and I'll be happy to. I'll meet you back here in fifteen; sound good?" She disappeared to her room to get ready.

Jack spied Daniel milling about the open space, talking with various citizens and trying to quell their fears. Still, it was

clear he was fearful himself—especially for Maddie if she were targeted for sacrifice, despite the Council's insistence to the contrary.

Jack was typically reserved and never one to pick a fight. Even in the face of Charlie's rage and staring down the barrel of a shotgun, Jack had kept his composure and tried to make peace. Now, he approached Daniel filled with an anger he wasn't used to. "Don't you ever touch my daughter again! Understand?"

Daniel met Jack's aggression with his own. "You don't belong here. If it weren't for Rose, I'd be personally escorting you out!"

"My wife, Sam's mother, was one of you—Tahltan. Sam is Tahltan. She is a princess of your people and far more powerful than your daughter." Throwing Daniel's own words in his face felt good, though there was some shame in discrediting a child.

"I don't see a crown. And leave Maddie out of this. She will not be handed to those monsters. Sam, though, would not be missed."

Jack was steaming, and before he realized what he was doing, his arm was in motion. His swing missed as Daniel sidestepped him and sent him tumbling to the ground, out of control. "Leave, and do not come back." Daniel walked away. Jack dusted himself off and let the self-pity of his defeat sink in.

Behind the locked fifteen-foot-tall Chamber doors, Rose and the other four council members were deep in discussion about how to solve their impossible quandary. To sacrifice anyone, let alone a child, was murder. The Tahltan revered nature, and to kill any living creature—except for sustenance—was frowned upon, unacceptable.

Rose led the discussion. "Councilmember Ezerza, what do you say? Your family has been in the valley as long as mine. Your father was tribe shaman when the original treaty was brokered between my own father and the Ijiraq." Lee Ezerza had followed his father's footsteps; he was now chief shaman of the tribe, and the second eldest member of the council, to Rose. Despite Rose's superior abilities, she yielded to Lee often on otherworldly matters—it happened more often than most tribe members knew.

"I have an idea that should satisfy the Ijiraq, but likely only temporarily. Perhaps a few years at best, but certainly not the eighty they expect."

"Go on . . ."

Jack said nothing to Sam about the scuffle with Daniel. He pushed his thoughts to Nan and the rock to avoid his

daughter's habitual mind reading. Sam led him to the first *inuksuk*, where he knelt to examine it. Always the scientist, Jack wanted to solve the rudimentary system of navigation. Sam took away his joy with a simple explanation and an urge to keep pressing forward.

The forest looked vastly different in the daylight, but Sam could still trace her steps from the previous night's trek. The melting snow made their path slick but allowed them to follow the trail between rock formations far more easily, and faster than Sam had just hours earlier.

"There!" Sam spied the boulder and realized she had been on the correct path laid out by the *inuksuk*—the next of which sat thirty yards past the giant rock. She hadn't been lost or disoriented by an Ijiraq. This brought her comfort, but also disappointment, that perhaps she wasn't as close to Ijiraq territory as she'd hoped.

The locket was still in the divot where she left it. Sam picked up the gold chain from the base of the boulder where it had fallen.

"Do you think Mom made the locket from this rock?"

Jack shrugged. Nan had never spoken of the locket's origins; he only knew it was special and something destined to end up with Sam.

The father-daughter duo couldn't contain their excitement.

"Go ahead, Dad."

"Are you sure?" Sam nodded.

Jack reached out and, as he'd done in Arizona, traced the embedded heart with trembling hands, confident that this was his wife's way of speaking to them. The marking began to glow, but not the familiar blue he had seen every other time. It was a brilliant shade of the most beautiful vermilion red. Like it did for Sam the night before, the heart pulsed to life. The winds didn't swirl as they expected, but there was a soft, beating glow, warm to the touch and full of life.

Jack pulled his hand back and the rock continued, just as bright. Sam was next, and as she touched the rock, the electric blue she was familiar with washed over the heart, still beating. "I can't believe what we're seeing," Jack said, stunned.

"Me either."

"Me either?" A familiar voice, the same one Sam heard as she ran from this place last night.

"Seriously, Ted? You followed me again? What's wrong with you?" She was incensed and raised her hands, a blue orb at the ready.

"No, please, not again. I just . . . I just wanted to say I'm sorry." Ted's apology seemed genuine, but Sam's reared-back stance was not accepting of his words.

"So you hiked all this way, tracking us, to tell me something you could have said back in the village?"

Jack recognized his daughter was not about to let the boy off so easily. "Son, unless you want to feel the wallop you almost got last night, I suggest you start talking. Sam,

lower your hands, please." Jack helped her, easing her from her riled state.

"I'll admit, I wanted to see the rock again, too. I want to know what it's all about."

"You want to know? Or your dad does?" asked Jack.

"He doesn't know I'm here. I swear. I'm sorry for causing such a commotion this morning. I tried waiting for you, Sam, I really did. I wanted to talk to Nana Rose with you, but my dad saw how shaken I was, and I was afraid for Maddie. When I saw the rock last night and the power you used . . . well, I needed to see it again. See if there was something that could save Maddie—that could save you too."

Sam took a moment to listen to Ted's thoughts, feeling his heart beating through his chest. He was telling the truth and had just wanted to help. She could also tell he was crushing hard and wanted to get back into her good graces. Her thoughts turned to Tommy and hoped he was still as enamored as this kid, hopefully more. She wasn't about to let on she was mildly smitten by him, but she would never let anything come between her and Tommy. Besides, Ted might be a tribal cousin. She felt a sudden upheaval in her stomach, which she promptly tamped down.

Sam let down her guard without accepting the apology and turned back to the heart-shaped divot. "It's gone!" Just as it had at the waterfall and Ash's boulder, the heart had vanished, this time with the locket. No trace either ever existed. "Mom?"

"Sam, no!" Jack commanded.

It was no use; she blamed Ted for interrupting their time with the boulder—with Nan—and she expelled a fireball that hit Ted square in the chest, knocking him out cold. Jack rushed to the boy's side to make sure he was alive, to the consternation of Sam, whose eyes were still glazed in swirling cobalt madness.

Jack continued tending to the boy, but when he turned around . . . "Sam? Where are you? Get back here!"

She was gone.

Just as she had planned the previous night when she believed she was lost, Sam headed toward the river. She had no intention of letting her dad—and Ted, if he were still alive—follow her back the way they came. She needed time to cool off, to process what just happened, and it provided her a chance to learn the lay of the land, perhaps even cross paths with an Ijiraq, whom she could really take her anger out on.

Sam pushed her way through the thick brush and down the valley wall along a narrow ledge—an animal trail of some kind. Occasionally, the terrain would flatten out, and she'd make it a point to double back on her muddy, and sometimes snowy, tracks. She now knew Ted was a skilled tracker, and she didn't want him knowing where she'd been. She used her powers to melt some sections of snow to really throw him off of her trail.

Sam was roughly two-thirds of the way to the valley

floor, where she could take a sip from the Stikine River and finally rest. She was doubling back again, along a particularly muddy and slick section of the trail when she slipped. Sliding and tumbling down a steep hill, bushes and brambles scraped her face, her only protection the thick layer of clothes keeping her warm. She couldn't stop her momentum, but a tree at the bottom sure did.

She was knocked unconscious.

She was dreaming, and she knew it. A playful little river otter licked her face and nuzzled up next to her, keeping her warm. It was a pleasant dream, something she hadn't had in several weeks—before the dread of high school and periods had pushed her past her comfort zone. She was smiling and at peace, feeling the warmth of the sun through her entire body. She didn't want to wake up and hoped her alarm clock wasn't set.

Her furry friend wanted to frolic, though, and continued to lick her cheek and push its cold, wet nose into her neck to get her to comply.

Sam sat bolt upright, grabbing her head, which throbbed mercilessly. The late afternoon sun was blinding, and the realization set in that she'd been out cold for some time. She took stock of her surroundings and could see the broken branches and crushed bushes and flowers which

marked the long tumble. Sam had come to rest at the bottom of the ravine, only inches from falling in the icy river, which she never could have survived.

She crawled on her hands and knees to the edge of the river for a drink.

As she bent down further to scoop a drink into her mouth, she could see the roots of the tree which had stopped her, pushing out from the riverbank and dangling just above the water. Something caught her attention, and she quickly jumped back. *What was that? A fish? A bird? AN IJIRAQ?*

Something was watching her; Sam could feel it. She remained motionless, like a child hiding under a blanket from the bogeyman, searching the surrounding area for the creature lying in wait, hoping to know what, and where, it was. The picture was fuzzy. She could only see the river otter from her dreams. Whatever it was wasn't letting her in and made her more nervous that she was finally about to face the Ijiraq.

It scurried past her, a flash in the corner of her eye. Then it pounced, knocking her to her back and attacking her—the otter. Her fear was replaced by joy as the rambunctious animal licked and pawed at her. It hadn't been a dream at all. This little fella had tended to her until she came to.

The animal made it hard for her to sit back up, but she managed to overpower it just enough to do so. "Hello to

you too, little one." The little river monster cheeped and chirped, sounding more like a bird than a mammal, as she patted it on the head. "Can I get that drink now?"

The slender animal slinked and slid into the icy water, showing Sam the way to her refreshment. She bent down for a scoop of water when it emerged from the depths and squirted her in the face with a mouthful of water. She wanted that drink so desperately, but she just sat back laughing at the otter's antics.

"Thank you for taking care of me, little one, but I need to get home. Can you show me the way?" Communication with the otter was reminiscent of her first encounters with Ash—there was a language barrier, yet she knew what it was saying and what it wanted her to do.

The critter dove back into the river, flipping onto its back, floating with the current. She could see the slight outline of a trail along the banks and had to run to keep pace. She was closer to the village than she'd known, less than a mile from where the road met the river at the entrance to Telegraph Creek. Somehow, her fall down the ravine had taken her right over and past the road. She felt lucky to be alive . . . she wondered if Ted was, too.

Before she returned to face the music and learn of the damage she'd done to Ted, she took one more moment of peace and thanked the creature one last time. "I hope we meet again, but perhaps next time under different circumstances." It crawled out of the river and pranced into her waiting arms for one last wet, icy kiss. The otter hopped up and down on all fours in a display of appreciation. "You're quite the puckish one, aren't you? Puck . . . hmm . . . I think I'll call you Puck. Sound okay to you?" The otter hopped higher, eventually tripping itself up and falling backward into the river, causing Sam to roar with laughter. Puck resurfaced, and spit a stream of water toward her, then chirped its approval. "Don't be a stranger, now."

Sam turned toward the village with her head down.

A punishment of some sort was waiting for her.

CHAPTER EIGHT

S am, where are you?" She could hear her dad's plea; he was back in the village, but she refused to answer. She snuck back to her room without being noticed, trying to remain hidden. The streets were barren, except for a few kids hanging from the jungle gym on the modest playground. They were lost in their own world of fun.

Her stomach, though, she couldn't ignore—Sam was famished. She pulled the only sustenance she had from deep within her backpack, an old granola bar that had probably been there since their life-altering trip to the Mogollon Rim. Sam bit through the stale oats anyway, grinding away on the now flavorless snack.

As guilt started to consume her, her appetite dwindled fast. Sam chucked the remainder of the bar across the room, knocking one of the old pictures off the wall, glass strewn everywhere. It made enough noise that within seconds there was a knock on her door. *Go away, Dad.*

"Honey, are you in there? Are you okay? Please, open

the door; we need to talk." Jack's voice was calm and tender; understanding, even. She opened the door, letting the slightest crack of early evening light through, and retreated to her bed. Sam's head was buried in her pillow before Jack could enter. "Sam, we need to talk about what happened. Ted, he . . . "

She refused to look up, preferring the suffocating embrace of the pillow against her face. Her muffled voice was barely audible. "Is he ok?"

"He needs you, Sam."

A flood of panic-stricken voices came rushing in. Daniel, Maddie, Nana Rose . . . Mr. Ezerza. It was the shaman she heard the clearest. "There's nothing else I can do. I'm sorry, Daniel." Then, sobbing—wails of grief overwhelming Sam's senses.

"They'll kill me if they see me. Offer me up to the Ijiraq, without question."

"I'll be right by your side, Princess. We can't avoid this any longer. Please, you can help him."

"He's gone, Dad. Dead." Jack knew the boy had been hanging on by the barest of threads. Sam screamed into her pillow, a gut-wrenching howl that shook Jack to his core. She had never made such an anguished sound, even at the life-altering news of losing her mother. But then, that hadn't been by her hand.

Ash would be ashamed—an understatement, no doubt. She had used her powers to kill, even if unintentionally. She

was powerful and out of control, and she knew it.

"Let's go, Sam. I promise, everything will work out. Nana Rose and I won't let anything happen to you." Sam didn't believe him. She could feel their pain and anger surging within her.

Sam raised her head enough to be clearly heard above her pillow soaked with tears. "I need to see him alone. No Daniel. No Maddie. No one, not even Nana."

"I'll see what I can do." Jack shut the door, leaving Sam in her grief, and headed toward the town's medical facility.

Jack reached the dirty white building with the faded red cross painted near the entrance. It was the only signage, and the agony greeted him before he stepped through the door. A window from the hall gave Jack a glimpse into the room. He remained out of sight, though from his angle, he could make out Ted's lifeless legs, the back of Lee Ezerza's head, and Rose, who stood at the boy's feet facing Jack. He was relieved that neither Daniel nor Maddie could see him. Although he had carried Ted over his shoulder well over a mile back to the village, he doubted Daniel would show him any grace or gratitude, given the outcome.

Jack waved a meek hand to get Rose's attention. She excused herself from the mourners without any undue attention to Jack's presence, and they proceeded outside to talk in private. The old woman nodded and returned inside; Jack made his way back to Sam.

Twilight had given way to dark skies, and Jack watched from near their rooms. A dirt-smeared panel of windows lined the hallway; the lights inside the hallway had burned out, and he was able to watch without fear of being seen as the group walked from the medical station and retired to the tribal hall.

"It's time, Princess."

Sam wasn't feeling much like a princess, but didn't possess the strength to respond. She only wanted to get to Ted, and hoped that her powers could save him . . . save them both.

They entered the facility, and Jack pointed to the room but remained in the hallway, as she'd requested. She had to do this alone.

Ted's body was covered head to toe by a faded blue sheet. Sam knew he was under there. Her heart raced, her mind transporting her back to that moment when she lost all control. She searched his mind for any sign of life, of thoughts—*perhaps he's just sleeping*. Sam willed him to wake up, but Ted's corpse lay lifeless.

She could see her dad through the hall window, nodding his support and belief that she could make this right. The slight push was what she needed to put aside her fears and begin the ritual.

Sam approached the bedside, thankful for the covering sheet. However, she was imagining Ted underneath: blank expression, eyes open, all color drained

from his face, and the burned flesh where she'd hit him with the fireball. She examined the sheet where it covered the boy's chest, praying to see it rise and fall, even slightly. But nothing. No life existed in that body.

Sam wiped her eyes after a few drops fell onto the sheet. She hadn't realized she was crying. Composing herself as best she could, Sam brought her hands together, formed a blazing sapphire orb of energy, and let it sit over Ted's heart. Eyes closed, she pushed the sphere through the sheet and down into his chest. The resistance was unnerving, but she continued until it was fully absorbed by the body. Her hands remained steady and continued to radiate as she willed his life force to return. What she'd done for the deer a few days earlier was nothing compared to this.

After ten minutes of uninterrupted concentration, Sam pulled her hands back and waited, focusing on Ted's chest, searching for any sign of movement.

Nothing.

She searched his thoughts, hoping for a glimmer of life.

Silence.

Her tears resumed, and she ran to her dad, burying her face. "I couldn't help, Dad. I couldn't save him."

"I'm sorry, Sam." Jack didn't know what else to say.

She needed the embrace and nothing else. No words of comfort, just the safety of her father's arms.

Tears rolled down Jack's face, as well—not for the lost child, but out of fear for his daughter's fate. She had killed another human being. Her life would never be the same.

Jack continued to hold Sam close as they made their way from the building back to their rooms. Sam did not want to be alone that night and requested he stay with her. The desire wasn't for comfort or company, but for safety. She was worried that Daniel or Maddie, or any other distraught member of the tribe might come looking to rip her from her bed and make her stand trial for Ted's murder.

The morning came faster than Sam had hoped. The thought of sleeping in to avoid an angry mob was far more pleasant. The dank, dimly lit room seemed appropriate—cell-like—where she assumed she'd be locked away soon enough. After crying herself to sleep, on waking, the tears resumed.

Jack slept, but was awoken by what sounded like the entire tribe shouting in the common. Sam, too, was shaken from her thoughts, but didn't dare eavesdrop on the crowd, not wanting to hear what fate they had in store for her.

The sounds grew louder and closer. Jack grabbed Sam and pulled her close, protecting her from the inevitable . . . *Knock, knock, knock.*

"Sam, dear? It's Nana; please open the door."

Sam and Jack remained still, not answering and hoping she'd go away and perhaps come back later, alone.

"Please, Sam. You need to come with me. There is nothing to fear."

She could feel her grandmother's protective aura through the door and breathed a calming breath.

Jack assured her, "Go ahead. I'm right here with you."

Sam opened the door, but Nana was not the only one there to greet her. "Ted? But . . . "

Nana Rose chuckled her usual chuckle, overjoyed by the moment, even though Sam and Jack couldn't believe their eyes. Ted looked no worse for wear and beamed a bright, vivid smile.

Sam leapt at him and wrapped her arms tight around his neck. "You're alive?!" It was a question and a statement.

"You saved me, Sam. I mean, you killed me, but then you saved me. Though, if you don't ease up with this hug . . ." Sam released herself from him and winced at the thought of her actions. "Too soon?" But the boy was all smiles, and the crowd that had come to excoriate her for her willful negligence . . . well, they were exuberant. What they had heard was a celebration.

"I'm sorry, Ted. I'm so, so sorry. I never meant for this to happen."

"And we're going to make sure it never does again, granddaughter. You and I have a lot of work to do. The more your power grows, the more restraint and control you will need to show," Nana said. "But first, we will feast, to celebrate this triumphant miracle made possible by your powers—even though it's a feast we would have rather not wanted." Rose made sure Sam understood the gravity of what she had done, and that despite the celebration and Ted's rebirth, it never should have happened to begin with. She needed Sam to recognize that. Though Sam had come so far since discovering her abilities, she was far from a master. She offered the girl a reassuring hug that things were going to be fine.

It was an unusually warm night, mere days removed from a snowstorm. A large bonfire was lit near the side entrance to the Great Hall ballroom, where the indoor festivities could spill out into the common. Men, women, and children danced, and laughed, and reveled.

Sam did her best to get in the mood, but she struggled to push aside the regret.

Person after person—an endless line of villagers— thanked her personally for saving Ted. She was ashamed but offered a humble "thank you" to each one in return— thankful for their grace and spirit of forgiveness. She hated being commended for fixing a problem that she had created. To say, "you're welcome" would have been accepting of praise she didn't deserve.

There was a noticeable absence from the party, however. Daniel and Maddie were ghosts. Perhaps a poor

choice of words, given that Ted had been one, even if briefly. Speak of the devil. She face-palmed at that thought.

"I know it's been a crazy day, but it's not that bad, is it?" Ted teased at her self-effacing gesture.

"I'm sorry, Ted. I'm not exactly comfortable being thanked for saving the boy I killed."

"Fair enough, but I'm going to thank you anyway."

"How are your dad and Maddie? They're conspicuously absent."

"Dad is thankful, though he may never show it. He still thinks you should be given to the Ijiraq, though, to ensure our peace and as penance for your actions. Maddie will be fine. She's just mad the attention isn't on her, especially with the coronation, and now having to share that with you." Ted placed a comforting hand on Sam's shoulder. "She'll get over it. They both will, but it may take some time. My dad may be the only person I've ever met that's more stubborn than you."

Sam shrugged off his hand, making him laugh. She finally smiled.

"There it is. I like that smile," Ted complimented. Sam blushed, and the boy noticed. "Would you like to dance?" He held out his hand, and she placed her hand inside his. If he could forgive her, then maybe she could learn to forgive herself.

"So we're agreed, then?" Rose asked the Council, who all concurred. They had slipped into the chambers away from the revelry and excitement, focused on ending the contract with the child-stealing monsters.

"This is your last chance to speak up. Once this is done, there is no going back," Rose said. More nodding followed. "Then let it be known and written into the tribal record that I, Rose Melia, leader and eldest of the Telegraph Creek Band of the First Nations of Tahltan, will be sacrificed to the Ijiraq, for the sake of our people and homeland."

"Send the messenger at once," Lee Ezerza commanded to the lowest ranking member of the council. The councilmember hastily exited the chambers, carrying a sealed envelope affixed with the tribal logo stamped in black wax. As he opened the door, a heavy thud—a child was sent flying across the foyer, causing him to drop the letter. He didn't know she was standing outside, and little did she know that the council would have been in session at such a time.

"I'm so sorry, Maddie. I didn't see you there. Are you okay?"

"Yes, sir," she said, rubbing her shoulder. "I guess I didn't know anyone was in there. I had to get away from the party and was looking for a quiet space. I'm sorry."

"No need to be; it was certainly my fault. Well, I should be going. Very important work to do." The councilmember was anxious to fulfill his task, and after helping Maddie up, made for the exit.

"I think you've forgotten something," Maddie said, handing him the letter.

"Oh my, yes. Thank you." And the man was on his way.

Maddie waited a few minutes before heading home. Her head was spinning from the conversation she'd overheard. She had thought it odd that the council was convening at such a late hour and followed to listen in, slipping into the enormous hearth to hide until they were behind closed doors. She spied on the festivities from the door between the foyer and the ballroom, hatching her plan to get back at Sam for what she'd put her brother through. Instead, she stumbled upon news she couldn't ignore.

CHAPTER NINE

*K*nock, knock, knock . . .

Sam faintly heard the tapping on her door, but it was the old woman's chuckle from the other side that woke her.

Nana Rose could hear rustling. "Sam, dear, it's time for you to begin your training."

"So early?" She wasn't ready to leave the comfort of her bed. Thoughts of dancing with Ted filled her head. She had enjoying the evening celebration after all, especially the company. Pangs of guilt welled as she checked the time on her phone and a picture of Tommy appeared—her wallpaper.

"I'll be right out, Nana."

"Meet me at the gazebo by the river. Ten minutes. There's not a moment to lose."

Time was running out. The coronation was less than a week away. Sam had no idea what she was even supposed to do to prepare. Nana was more intent on her training than ball gowns and tiaras. That suited Sam just fine. The pomp

and circumstance, all eyes on her, the girly dresses . . . *No thanks.*

As she was leaving her room, something caught her eye under the desk. Atop the desk was the broken picture frame she'd knocked off the wall; Jack had cleaned up the glass for her. However, the picture had come to rest under the desk where her dad must not have seen it. She picked it up, taking a quick glance before setting it down with the frame.

Something about the picture made her grab it and look again.

The photograph showed a gathering of some kind. Center-frame were two men, one wearing what Sam assumed were traditional Tahltan ceremonial robes, but it was the other man who caught her attention. He was dressed in an animal hide which came up and over his head, resembling . . . *a caribou?* There were no horns, but the expressionless eyes—their color was unmistakable in the black and white image.

Sam flipped the photo over, and a penciled inscription validated her guess: "Chief Melia agrees to 80-year peace accord. ~1941."

She looked at the picture one more time, and there she was, a four-year-old Rose standing in front of her father, his hand on her shoulder and her mother on the other side. She wore a smock which hung to her knees, where it met a pair of high tartan socks, and at her feet, peeking out from behind her tiny legs, *a river otter*. Curious. But more curious was what Sam spied dangling around young Rose's neck . . . *the locket!*

Sam pocketed the photo in hopes of gaining answers from Nana, and headed to the gazebo.

"You have a lot to learn, Sam. You cannot be so rash with your thoughts or actions, lest you will hurt someone again. You are a raven, so you must push aside the wantonness inherent in you. Learn to control your emotions and channel your negative feelings for good. Let the raven guide you . . . to help your people and shape your world." Nana's words were not falling on deaf ears, but there was so much meaning Sam was struggling to uncover. She felt like Luke, trying to make sense of Yoda's teachings in the bogs of Dagobah.

Sam couldn't take it any longer and interrupted Nana's teaching—the impetuousness she'd just asked Sam to control coming all too naturally. She pulled the picture from her pocket. "Nana, can you tell me about this?" She handed her the photo.

Nana dropped and shook her head, displeased with the interruption. With a sigh, she accepted Sam's curiosity, knowing the lesson couldn't continue until she did so. "A

fateful day," she sighed, examining the picture.

"The back says it's the day the tribe came to peace with the Ijiraq."

"Aye." She seemed to get lost in the memory of the day. The little girl in the picture, now a wrinkled old woman, wondering where the time had gone. "You have questions?"

"That's an Ijiraq in the picture . . . next to you, and your mother and father?"

Nana nodded. "In human form, yes. With its mouth covered, so not to scare the tribe members any more than they already had. A request by my father." Sam was so focused on the creature's eyes and the other elements in the photo that she hadn't noticed the vertical maw of the monster strategically covered by part of the hide.

"And the locket around your neck. Is that the same locket . . . ?" Sam grabbed at her chest where the necklace would have laid if it were still in her possession.

"Handed down for generations. I gave it to your mother on her sixteenth birthday, as I had received it from my mother, and her mother before that. It's unclear just how old it is, only that it was carved from a boulder in the forests about a mile from here. I was wearing the locket when I was taken. I wanted to tell you when I saw you wearing it, but it wasn't time. I believe *it* was responsible for my return. The Ijiraq were afraid at the sight of it—this fear is my only recollection of the time I was gone. That locket holds great power."

"So why not use it to force the Ijiraq to leave the tribe alone? Why agree to a deal to sacrifice a child?"

"It only protects the one who wears it. When I was abducted, the locket was tucked inside my parka and hidden from view. It wasn't discovered until I was brought to their den."

Sam was growing frantic, knowing the ageless rock pendant was no longer in her possession, fused to the boulder.

"Sam, there's no need to panic. The legend is coming true."

"Legend? What are you talking about?"

"You found the boulder, didn't you? It's why the locket no longer hangs around your neck where you kept it safe." Sam offered a confused but guilty look. "Legend says that the ancient ancestors of the Ijiraq came to this land to escape the persecution they had endured in their original homeland of Karavan. They were being hunted and wiped out by indescribable monsters. A Tahltan shaman was wandering the forests when he was attacked by one of these new creatures."

"An Ijiraq."

"Yes, and he was gravely injured. In his escape, the shaman stumbled upon a remarkable granite boulder which he hid behind. The Ijiraq found him but refused to go anywhere near the boulder, instead letting out a terrifying cry before running away. The shaman was safe but dying from his injuries. When he laid his hands on the giant rock, a wave of energy pulsated through him and his mortal wounds began to heal. It's said that he carved the heart-shaped pendant from the magic boulder and provided it to the daughter of the chief to protect her from any harm."

"I need to get the locket back! To protect us!"

"No, dear. It's no longer necessary."

"But . . . "

"The legend ends with instructions and a prophecy. The eldest daughter of the tribe is to receive her birthright upon turning sixteen years old. She must take the locket to the boulder from which it was derived, to reunite them. The ceremony is done alone and restores the protective properties of the locket for another generation. The prophecy, however, speaks of a mighty Tahltan princess who will return the heart-shaped rock for the last time. Upon doing so, the boulder will once again be whole, and the princess will lead the Tahltan people and banish the Ijiraq back to Karavan—back to their rightful home."

"You're saying I'm the prophesied princess?" Sam wasn't prepared for this.

"Did the rock and locket become one?" Nana's question was sarcastic, but Sam nodded. "Then yes, Sam, you are that princess meant to lead our people out of these dark times."

The news weighed heavy on her; she slid to the ground, a bit dizzy. Her thoughts were everywhere at once, questions coming and going, doing her best to not pass out. Nana Rose believed she was ready for such an extraordinary responsibility; Sam, not so much.

"I think perhaps we should get you back to your room. Rest for a while, and we will discuss this more later." Nana didn't want to push her any further. "We will resume your training after lunch."

Training took on a whole new meaning now. It was no longer only about controlling her powerful impulses, but leading an entire group of people toward the culmination of a prophecy, back to their freedom, and in the face of creatures' intent on destroying them at all costs.

Where is Karavan?

The door shut behind her before she could ask. Sam opened it again, but Rose had already disappeared, faster than a woman her age could have possibly moved. Sam hoped her dad was in his room, but he too, was nowhere to be found. Alone, she listened to Nana Rose's sage advice and lay down, surprisingly falling asleep despite her racing mind.

Knock, knock, knock . . .

Sam groaned. "Again? Just a few more minutes, Nana."

"Sam, get up now. There's a problem." It was her dad.

"Maddie is missing," he said through the door.

Sam wasn't a fan of Ted's younger sister, the near-constant glares and hateful thoughts she could hear, but, if what Nana said was true, she had a duty to her people—all of them, including Maddie.

Jack and Sam joined Rose and the rest of the council in the chambers, along with Daniel and Ted.

"What are they doing here? We don't need their help," said Daniel.

"We need all the help we can get," said Rose, and Daniel humphed. "Ted, do you know where your sister may have gone?" He shook his head, afraid of the possibilities. "Did she say anything to anybody? Anything out of the usual?"

"There is something,' said the lowest ranking councilmember. "When I left last night to meet with the messenger, I opened the chamber door and accidentally hit Maddie with the door. She was just outside."

Lee Ezerza said, "She was listening. She knows of our plan to deal with the Ijiraq. You don't think she would try and do something about it herself, do you?"

"That depends. What plan?" Sam said, confidently questioning the elder shaman. She was a natural leader, and Nana yielded that power to her granddaughter.

Rose explained, "I was to give myself to the Ijiraq in exchange for a few more years of peace. It was the only solution."

"Nana, no, you can't. There must be another way," Sam begged.

"I will not sacrifice you or Maddie. Though, I suspect she sacrificed herself when she learned of my intentions. You two are more alike than you know." It was a compliment, but Sam preferred not to be compared to her royal rival, especially now that she possessed the knowledge that she was the true leader of the tribe.

Sam asked, "Where is the messenger? If he delivered the message—this plan—to the Ijiraq, then they would know that Maddie is not the sacrifice. Maybe he knows something."

Rose motioned to the younger statesman to fetch the messenger, and he left immediately. "We'll see if the messenger knows anything, but they may believe we changed our minds and Maddie was surrendering herself. Eighty years of sustenance would surely not be turned down in favor of an old woman."

"But, we . . . she hasn't been crowned yet. She's not officially a princess yet." She was grasping for reasons.

"She, just like you, is royalty since birth. The coronation is a mere formality—a coming-out party that proclaims the coming-of-age of the next in the lineage of the royal Tahltan nation. The Ijiraq don't abide by our traditions. Crown or no, they only care that the sacrifice they receive is someone who will sustain their immortality for another eighty years."

"Immortality? I thought you said you weren't sure what they did with the stolen children?"

"I'm sorry, Sam. I should have told you. I didn't want to scare you, and that was before I learned that you are the chosen one."

Jack interjected, "What do you mean 'chosen one'?"

Nana recounted the legend for the group—Jack being the only one who never heard it before—though until now, no one in the council had known of the locket's homecoming.

Daniel's attitude toward Sam changed in an instant with the news. He was relieved; he never wanted that responsibility thrust upon his daughter. "I'm humbled to serve you, Dene Tsesk'iye. Whatever you need. I just want to get Maddie back." Sam was confused by the name, but there was no time for explanation. Nana chuckled, pleased with Daniel's instant acceptance of Sam as their new leader.

The doors burst open with the expectation that the councilmember had returned with the messenger. Instead, it was a frantic young woman, scared by what she was witnessing. They followed her to the common, where overhead, hundreds of ravens circled, cawing so loud they filled the valley with their echoes.

"Dene Tsesk'iye, they are here for you. They are here to protect us," said Daniel. "Protect us from the Ijiraq."

"I'm not so sure," responded Sam. She remembered what Nana had told her about the Ijiraq disguising themselves, often as ravens. They were too high to see their eyes, to verify the presence of the haunting ruby gaze of the creatures. Sam concentrated, hoping to hear something. The cawing was deafening, but she slowly pushed it from her mind and settled into a trance-like state.

"No more games! Death!" To her horror, Sam heard the words clearly repeating over and over, filling her head. She broke her concentration, having listened to the warning, and for fear of going mad.

"It's the Ijiraq, not ravens. They've come with a warning: Death. They think we're playing games by offering Nana but sending Maddie. They think it's a trick." It was more than what Sam had heard, but she understood the intent behind the warning. "Back inside," she commanded to the group. "Everyone, back in your homes now!" She yelled to anyone who could hear her.

Rose said, "We need to send another message to the Ijiraq. We need to let them know that Maddie was acting alone and our original offer still stands. Perhaps then, they will return her to us."

"Will they listen?" asked Jack.

"It's hard to say. They are a distrustful bunch, but I don't see any other way. If we can't make things right, they may not return her. It must be a one-for-one swap. I must give myself up to them immediately if we are to bring Maddie home."

The young councilmember finally returned and walked in alone, or so Sam thought. "Where's the

messenger?" The man looked down. From behind him appeared a soft brown creature, which chirped as soon as it laid eyes on Sam. "Puck?" The animal hopped sideways on all fours to Sam, allowing her to pick him up and pushing his cold, wet nose into her cheek. "You're the messenger?"

Nana chuckled to herself. "This little one has been our liaison to the Ijiraq since I was a little girl."

Sam pulled the old photo, which was still in her jacket pocket, and held it up to the otter. "This is you?" More chirps of approval.

"You know the messenger?" asked Ted.

She looked at Daniel, hoping her words wouldn't spark any anger. "After the incident at the boulder . . ." Daniel's demeanor remained unchanged, listening intently and hanging on every word from his chief. "After I ran away, I fell down a hill and was knocked unconscious. I landed near the river, and Puck nursed me back to health and then showed me the way back to the village."

Lee Ezerza spoke, "Puck is a trusted ally of the Tahltan. So much so that my father blessed him with the gift of longevity. He's quite the old man, despite his youthful vigor."

"But how do you know his name?" asked Ted.

"I thought I named him. He was so playful, so 'puckish' that it seemed fitting," Sam responded.

"That's exactly why your great grandmother named him that, all those years ago. Great minds think alike," Nana said, her chortle much louder than usual and providing the group a moment of levity.

The laughter died down quickly, however, as they returned to the task at hand. The council drafted a new letter and sealed it with the same black wax and tribal stamp as the first.

Sam provided Puck his mission plans. "Alright, little one, you're up to bat. Take this where it needs to go. And if you see Maddie, come right back and let us know." Puck gave an affirmative chirp, took the letter in his mouth, and waddled out the door, which Sam opened for him.

When the door closed, the others had a quizzical look on their faces—all except Jack and Nana. It was Ted who asked the question on everyone's mind. "You can talk to it? Understand it? I thought Puck was just a glorified carrier pigeon, trained to go back and forth."

"It's not so much that I can talk to him, but I can hear his thoughts and send him my thoughts. The spoken words were for your benefit, not his."

Ted raised an eyebrow, confused more by Sam's explanation, but he didn't question her any further. He trusted Sam knew what she was doing, and if his dad was okay with it, so was he.

There was nothing left to do but wait for Puck's return.

CHAPTER TEN

S am returned to the boulder and lamented the disappearance of the heart. She needed her mom. She needed guidance. The forest was a cold, dark maze and she didn't know which way to go. Puck, who knew the way, never returned. She would do the only thing she could, continue to follow the *inuksuk* in hopes of it leading to the Ijiraq . . . to Maddie. *Stupid girl.*

It was unclear whether Maddie gave herself up to save Nana or if the Ijiraq stole her for her youth and powers, angered by the perceived games. Sam certainly preferred Maddie to be the offering over her grandmother. *Let her sacrifice herself.* Sam wasn't ready to lose Rose. She had many questions about her mother and the tribe, especially now that she was their leader. Besides, Maddie would just be a thorn in her side. She couldn't imagine the girl would accept her authority, even if Daniel did.

Sam pushed further into the forest, her thoughts turning to the otherworldly place her grandmother had

spoken of—*Question #1 when I get back: Ask Nana Rose about Karavan.* What indescribable monsters could be so horrifying that even the Ijiraq had to escape? *Monsters that frighten monsters.* It sent a shiver down her spine.

Sam wandered from one stacked rock pile to the next, deeper into the woods where the moonlight failed to shine, and temperatures continued to drop. Her eyes darted through the trees, searching for signs of the Ijiraq, perhaps a settlement or village of some sort. Two hours of traversing through the forest had left her cold and lost.

She checked her phone: 1:00AM. She had five hours to get back before anyone would realize she had sneaked out and taken matters into her own hands. At least she didn't have Ted following her this time. She looked behind her, searching for his thoughts . . . Nothing. She was alone.

Then she heard it. The noises pushed into her head directly in front of her. It was a weak signal, but enough that she could follow. She was getting close, but to what, she didn't know. It wasn't voices she was following, more like grunts and groans—an animal of some type, asleep in a den. The nearer she got, the louder her head rang. Not one. Not two. A pack of animals nearly one hundred strong, was close by.

Sam slowed her pace. Every footstep was calculated to not awaken whatever horrific dreamers she was about to encounter. She knew good and well it was the Ijiraq, and she needed to get as close as possible without waking them, or they'd rip her apart.

A rustling approached from behind her, followed by the chatter of a familiar friend. She knew before she turned around. "Puck, am I glad to see you," she whispered. He responded with a few more chirps, too loud for Sam's comfort. "Shh. Keep it down, or you'll get us caught." Sam decided to try telepathy. She was hopeful that, as with Ash, it would allow her to translate his cute otter sounds into something they could both understand.

Do you understand me? Sam asked, and Puck bobbed his head up and down. *Okay, good. How close are we to the Ijiraq camp?*

Puck chirped an audible chirp, and Sam shushed him once again.

Think about your answer, but don't make a sound! She wasn't sure she was getting through to the little guy, despite another affirmative head bob.

It didn't matter; a heavy snap interrupted them. Sam turned, and a massive creature hovering over eight feet tall, with gnarled horns and flashing red eyes, let out a death scream from its vertical mouth. Rows of razor-sharp teeth glinted in a perfect stream of moonlight through the trees. It was salivating as if it had just found its meal.

Sam was frozen in fear as the beast made its move. She'd never seen something so ghastly, so utterly frightening, that she forgot who she was and what she was capable of. It was coming directly at her, horns first. Sam curled up in a ball, hands over her head, waiting for the inevitable . . . but it never came.

The Ijiraq howled and shook the earth as it bounded away. Sam began to unfurl herself, but there was no sign of what had caused the monster to flee. Puck slithered up to check on her and make sure she wasn't injured. *"Did you . . . ? But, how?"* Sam couldn't understand how her cute and cuddly new friend could have fended off such a vicious beast.

Puck squeaked softly with his fishy otter breath. *You're okay; I scared him. Told him to go away or I'd be mad. Then I bit his ankle! Big oaf is always causing trouble.* Sam could hear Puck, clear as day.

You what? Wait . . . you can talk? Sam asked, still confused but grateful for Puck's bravery. *He could have hurt you.*

Him? Hurt me? Not possible. Puck's too quick for that one. He's a sentry. Guarding the Ijiraq home.

How close are we? Sam asked, taking note of the unusual cadence of the otter's "voice" — reminiscent of a particular Star Wars character who also liked to talk about himself in the third person, though Puck was adorable.

So close. Just over the ridge, there. Puck pointed to the top of the hill, two hundred yards away.

Sam began to make her way to the ridge, to gather intelligence and hopefully, find Maddie.

Careful. Nagha indeed is warning the others. Your presence

will be known. And they'll know Puck helped you.

I just want to get a quick peek. I need to know what we're up against. Did you deliver the message? What did they say?

Say? They say nothing. They only mad. Think it's a trick.

Sam and Puck reached the top of the hill. A few torches illuminated the Ijiraq camp, just enough to make out a sprawling community. Twenty large tents—ten on each side, lining a central clearing—made up the bulk of the town. Several baskets of goods fronted three smaller tents which appeared to be two stores and a medical station. The Ijiraq were beginning to wake and exit their tents at Nagha's insistence that a Tahltan spy was nearby.

Antlers and blood-red eyes gleamed everywhere in the firelight. She could see what she assumed to be women and children, based on the size of their horns and their smaller statures. Others were built like Nagha: hulking beasts which towered above the others—soldiers and sentries.

Finally, an older-looking Ijiraq with a hunched carriage and tired appearance, hobbled to the center of the clearing with the aid of an ancient-looking staff—their leader, according to Puck. The elder began speaking to his people, unintelligible to Sam but filled with vitriol—hate. One word was understood: Maddie. The Ijiraq burst out in screams, raising fists and weapons in the air. The echoes of their raucous eruption filled Sam's head. She couldn't recuse herself from the sights and sounds, horrific as they were.

What are they saying, Puck?

It's not good, Tsesk'iye. There was that word again, the same name Daniel had called her after learning she was the chosen leader of the Tahltan. *The Ijiraq Dene says they are going to perform the immortality ceremony tomorrow. They say Maddie will be the sacrifice and give them life for another eighty years. They celebrate.*

Dene? The chief? Puck nodded. *We need to get Maddie out of there.*

Puck agrees, and we must warn all of the attack.

What attack? I thought you said this was just their sacrifice ceremony?

That it is, Tsesk'iye, but then they will attack. Ijiraq will make an example of Tahltan for playing tricky games.

Why do you keep calling me 'Tsesk'iye'? Daniel called me that, as well. Even called me Dene Tsesk'iye.

You are the Tahltan Raven Chief. The one who will free your people from the cursed peace. Puck thinks Ijiraq won't like that very much. No sacrifice, no immortality.

Raven Chief had a nice ring to it, but Sam's focus on protecting the Tahltan—saving Maddie and stopping the attack—pushed her to depths she never expected. Deep cobalt filled her eyes, nearly black.

Sam kept her next thought to herself: *I guess they'll have to be disappointed and learn to die like everything else in this world.* This was no longer about just saving her people; it was about eradicating an evil from the world by starving them of what they needed most. The Ijiraq would not steal another life force.

What do we do next? asked Puck.

We get Maddie. Follow me.

Puck slinked behind Sam, doing his best to keep up as they flanked the Ijiraq village until they were within feet of the medical tent, but well hidden in the brush. Sam searched her mind listening for signs of Maddie, but nothing came through. She had either been knocked unconscious or slept so deeply that Sam couldn't even pick up on her dreams. She assumed the former—with as much noise as these ghastly creatures made, nothing could possibly sleep.

Puck, can you get under the tent to see if Maddie is in there? The otter bobbed his head. *Be careful . . . and quiet,* Sam instructed.

Puck slipped his head under the tent for a look around. Sam watched as his tiny, headless body pranced from side to side, waiting for his affirmative transmission that Maddie was inside. He pulled his head back out and shook it from side to side. Sam wanted him to stay quiet, and he was doing a good job.

Check the smaller tents. She wasn't convinced Maddie would be there—where the Ijiraq kept their goods—but she had to be sure. The princess-in-waiting was more likely in a larger tent, guarded by others of Nagha's ilk.

Sam stalled in hopes of formulating a plan that didn't involve a firefight. *Get in. Get Maddie. Get out.* It was the best she could conceive under pressure. With any luck, they'd be halfway back to Telegraph Creek before anyone knew she had disappeared—just enough time to warn of what would surely be a swift retaliation.

A few moments later, Puck returned, confirming what she already knew. They made their way along the larger tents on the near side of the encampment, each time Puck sneaking in for a peek and each time returning with disappointing news. Maddie was being held on the other side of the camp, likely in the Dene's tent.

I have an idea. They know you, right? Puck nodded and let out a small chirp. *And Nagha knows you're nearby. I need you to distract them. Tell them that I returned to the village to warn them. That we are preparing for battle and going to march on this camp at dawn.*

Puck was confused. *Tsesk'iye, will that not make them even more angry? Surely they will attack if they think Tahltan prepare for war.*

If they believe that we will attack first, they will assume we are bringing the fight to them. I'm banking that they will stop prepping for the ceremony and start fortifying their defenses. While they're scrambling, I will sneak around the other side and slip Maddie out. No Maddie, no sacrifice. And they will be here waiting for an attack that will never happen. After they realize we're not coming, it should give the tribe time to prepare for an Ijiraq invasion.

Puck understood but was hesitant. He was worried for

Sam's safety and that of the Tahltan. They were no longer the warriors that their ancestors once were. They were peaceful and avoided conflict at all costs. It was why they had succumbed to the eighty-year sacrifice. One life was a trade they were willing to endure to maintain peace and avoid war.

I will let you know once I've located Maddie. I'll need you to distract the guards and keep them occupied, so they don't realize she's gone.

Puck understands and will do his best. Be careful, Dene.

Puck returned to the top of the ridge, entering camp from where they had encountered Nagha. He waddled halfway down the hill before tumbling the rest of the way, head over feet—a grand entrance which more than sufficed, allowing Sam to pass to the other side of the village unseen. She was unsure just how much of Puck's efforts were an act and how much was genuine clumsiness. Either way, it created the diversion Sam needed.

Sam could see him—and hear him—as she made her way across the wide gap at the far end of the makeshift village. He was saying all the right things, though Sam didn't have time to continue listening. She had to keep pushing forward.

A deep bugle blared and echoed through the trees, made by a sentry blowing through what appeared to be the cut horn of one of their own—the Ijiraq were preparing for war. Her plan was working, and it was her signal to begin searching the tents.

It didn't take long to find her target; Maddie was in the third tent Sam checked. Her back rested against a large, vertical, wooden post, hands tied behind her, ankles too. Her head was slumped over, and her breathing shallow. Two guards were posted inside, thankfully faced toward the entrance, or she would have been spied for sure.

Puck. Third tent from the back. I'm in, Sam transmitted.

Sam crawled through the backside of the yurt, slipping behind a stack of boxes, though not as quiet as she'd hoped. As she propped herself up, a can that sat on top of the boxes rattled. One of the sentries turned, the crunching dirt underneath its giant hooves drawing closer. The shadow of its twisting rack grew larger on the back of the tent as it neared.

I need you now, Puck!

On cue, the tent flap opened, pulling the guard from his investigation. "What do you want, Deyo?" asked the guard. "You don't belong here." The three began speaking in the Ijiraq language, which Sam couldn't decipher. Something was amusing, as they all roared in laughter before they exited, leaving Maddie alone.

Puck draw them away. All is clear, Dene Tsesk'iye.

Thank you! Sam was taken aback by Puck's ability to speak to the Ijiraq in their own tongue. Why did they call him Deyo? And what was so funny? The questions only slowed her down. There would be plenty of time to

interrogate Puck when they were all safe.

Sam beelined it to the unconscious girl and rather enjoyed slapping her face a few times to wake her. It was working, so she slapped her harder. "Shh. Don't make a sound, or we're both dead."

"What?" replied a groggy Maddie.

"Shh!"

Sam searched for a knife to cut the ropes, but came up empty. She had wanted to avoid using her powers to burn through the knots and create any type of smoke or scent that would signal her presence. She didn't have a choice. She grabbed the thick braided rope in both hands and didn't let go. Smoke began to swirl as the ropes disintegrated.

"Where are we?" Maddie asked.

Sam didn't hide her anger with the annoying simp, who had clearly gotten in over her head. She placed a firm hand over Maddie's mouth. "I said BE QUIET. Or they'll hear us."

Maddie let out a muffled squeal as her lips and mouth burned under Sam's still-hot hands.

"What's going on in there?" A passing Ijiraq heard the commotion, but more likely Maddie's inability to shut up.

"We have to go, now!" Sam wasn't so quiet anymore—there didn't seem to be a need. "Hurry, under the tent."

Sam led Maddie to where she had initially entered and held the bottom of the tent so the pair could escape: Maddie first, then Sam, who was halfway through before she was grabbed by the ankle and dragged backward.

"Maddie, run! Get home now! Use the *inuksuk*!"

Sam was lifted off the ground, upside down like a rag doll, and found herself face-to-face with another of the menacing monsters. Bigger than Nagha, it held her high. She could smell the hot, rotten stench of its breath covering her face and crawling up her neck.

"Going somewhere?" asked the Ijiraq, with a horrifying sideways smile. She could understand it—it spoke English.

"Going home," Sam replied, and the beast laughed a hearty laugh.

Sam pulled her hands together and formed a fireball more massive than she ever had—a basketball-sized orb of swirling blue, green, and white flames. It surprised even her. She launched it at her captor, hitting him square in the chest, and sent her plummeting to the ground head first. The earth shook as his body hit the floor. Sam jumped to her feet, standing over the caribou-like ogre, a hole burned through its chest. She could see the ground through the other side of the bloody carnage.

Sam had killed, yet again.

As she stood over the body—victorious against this evil—she failed to notice the tent doorway filled with another hellacious savage bearing down on her.

A sharp pain across the back of her head preceded the blackness.

CHAPTER ELEVEN

Maddie! What happened?" asked Daniel.

The shaken young girl stumbled into town having used the *inuksuk* to guide herself home, as Sam had instructed. She was incoherent, still confused by her experience with the Ijiraq.

"Sam . . ." she mumbled before falling unconscious into her father's arms.

Daniel yelled for help. It was barely dawn and most people were still asleep, or at least inside. It took only seconds for the masses to rush to his aid—Jack was first.

"Let's get her inside. I'll get Mr. Ezerza and Rose," Jack said.

By the time Jack had exited Daniel's home, the council was already outside waiting. Lee Ezerza proceeded inside to examine Maddie.

"Where is Sam?" asked Rose.

"Not here, but I can lobby a guess. Maddie mentioned Sam's name before she passed out," said Jack.

"Send for the messenger," Rose requested. "Puck may have answers. He is an Ijiraq, after all."

"I'm sorry, what?" said Jack. "The otter . . . it's one of them?"

A grumbling din of questions and concern built among the gathered crowd. Puck's true identity had only ever been known to the council.

Rose hushed the crowd and explained how Puck, whose birth name was Deyo, had been banished from the Ijiraq. He had grown weary of taking the lives of innocent children just to satisfy a desire for immortality. When the eighty-year truce was negotiated, Deyo had lobbied on the side of the Tahltan, betraying his father, the Ijiraq Dene. He believed they could find other ways to increase their lifespan or even remain immortal. His disloyalty should have gotten him killed, but Rose's father had requested that he become the official messenger between the tribes, though he was no longer allowed to live with his own people.

The Tahltan, also, did not fully trust him, so he was forced to live alone. Lee Ezerza's father ceremoniously granted Deyo longevity without the need for sacrifice and removed the ever-present red glow from his eyes. Though, to do so, he would have to give up his Ijiraq form and forever take on that of a creature of his choosing. The only son of the Ijiraq Chief chose to live as an otter, confined to the Stikine River, where he would remain anonymous to anyone. He felt free, and his joyous new outlook on life earned him his new name: Puck.

Most of the day had passed, and Maddie was finally beginning to awake. Puck had still not arrived, and the council was unsure if he ever would. Sam was also still missing, but Jack was confident in his daughter and her ability to protect herself with her powers. Rose, however, was keenly aware of just how dangerous the Ijiraq were, despite those powers.

Rose, Jack, and Daniel gathered around Maddie's bed. Ted remained outside but within earshot, pretending not to eavesdrop. He was instructed to stay away, but he needed to know what was happening—especially with Sam.

"I'm sorry, Nana Rose. I couldn't let you sacrifice yourself, so I found the Ijiraq and gave myself up. I thought I was strong enough, that I could survive," said a still weak Maddie.

"And what of Sam?" Rose asked.

Maddie caressed her bruised cheek. "I'm not sure. I just remember she untied me and helped me escape, but she was dragged back into the tent." Tears started to well. "I ran. When I got to the top of the ridge, I looked back and saw a massive flash from inside. I should have gone back and tried to help her."

Daniel spoke, "You did the right thing, or you both would be captured now."

Maddie wasn't so sure and looked apologetically to Jack.

Jack nodded, "Your dad is right. Don't worry, we will get her back."

"Is there anything else you can tell us, child?" said Rose, and Maddie shook her head.

Ted had heard enough. He slipped away unnoticed.

"There is one more thing," Maddie remembered. "They kept me asleep, but I'm not sure how."

Rose said, "Surely they are doing the same to Sam. They know who has powers and who doesn't. They can read your thoughts, sense your fears, and they use this to control you. As powerful as you and Sam are, they had to keep you knocked out to contain you. They know you are the princesses and that you can destroy them if they are not careful."

"So I am powerful enough?"

"Yes, dear, but you were not prepared and should never have gone out on your own. Sam is in far graver danger. She is stronger than any of us, but she is naive in the ways of the Ijiraq."

Despite her fear for Sam, a look of jealousy crossed Maddie's face. She had hoped to save her people but was helpless, despite her abilities.

Jack's demeanor changed as well, his confidence in his daughter waning with each revelation about the Ijiraq.

"Mom?" said Sam. Her eyes were blurry, but she couldn't rub them into focus with her hands tied behind her back. She shook her head, but her mother's soft brown eyes and warm smile were still staring back at her. *This has to be a dream.*

Sam looked down and could see the blood and entrails, what was left of the Ijiraq she'd splattered throughout the tent. She yanked her shoulders from side to side to loosen her binds. Her ankles were tied tight, as well. When she looked up, the vision of her mother was gone. *Definitely a dream.*

She kept struggling to free herself before remembering how she had unshackled Maddie. Her hands started to glow, but they were taped palm to palm, her ability to create a fireball inhibited.

"I'd suggest against that," said a gruff voice from behind her.

"Let me go, or you'll end up like your friend!" Sam threatened. Blue energy surrounded her and her eyes glazed over, but she could not release it and incapacitate her captor.

The creature stepped from the shadows and revealed himself. It was Nagha. "You may want to calm down, or I'll do it for you."

Sam ignored his warning and continued to struggle.

Nagha let out a sinister laugh, reaching out a hoof to touch the energy field. A spark jumped, giving the beast a slight shock, and he laughed harder. "I guess you're a real firecracker, huh? This is your last warning. Let down your guard, or I'll let it down for you."

Sam realized she was defenseless, and the blue force began to dim.

"That's a good girl." She wanted to rip into him, tear him in two. "Thanks for your sacrifice. We'll live for another thousand years on just you alone." Nagha's tone was smug and condescending. "Though, as far as I'm concerned, we'll still need another of your kind in eighty years. I suppose that's up to Dene."

"Good thing you're not Chief then."

"You're a feisty one. I like that. It'll make it that much more pleasurable to feel your energy surging through me after tomorrow's ceremony."

"Not a chance, creeper!" Her hands were glowing white-hot and her eyes glazed over, again.

Nagha let out another belly laugh, reared back, and cracked Sam across the head, knocking her back into dreamland.

Ted could hear the commotion as he reached the top of the ridge, peeking at the sight of the Ijiraq scrambling to gather

weapons and supplies. He had only seen an Ijiraq once before, when he was four years old — the memory would stick with him forever. It gave him pause, considering his next move might bring him face-to-teeth with the creature which had haunted him throughout his childhood. His heart raced and he could feel a wave of anxiety wash over him, remembering how he had wandered from his mother while out picking berries not too far from this area.

A young Ijiraq with less than five points on its rack had grabbed him. If the monster's escape hadn't brought them across Ted's mother's path, he would have disappeared forever. With a swiftness Ted had never seen from his mom, she reached out in desperation, her arm pierced through by one of the razor-sharp horns. It caused the creature to drop him and gallop away with his mother. It was the last time he ever saw her.

Ted was in over his head, nearly petrified in his thoughts, when a message snapped him to attention. *Help me, Ted.*

"Sam? Is that you? Where are you?" The only response was a sharp pain shooting through his left temple.

He dragged himself up over the ledge once again, searching for signs of his friend. He did his best to push out the fright, knowing he owed Sam his life and desiring to save hers. Scenes of a knight rescuing the damsel in distress skipped in and out of his thoughts — a selfish idea of earning her love and adoration.

After taking account of the Ijiraq preparations—"Information is power," he could hear his dad say—Ted launched his ingress into the shallow valley and positioned himself behind a dense cluster of evergreens on the far side of the encampment. It placed him close to the rear tents, but far enough away from where the Ijiraq were mustering that he could sneak in unseen.

He examined the backside of the tents nearest his location. A trail led from one as if something, or someone, had dragged itself from underneath. He moved in line with the path, careful to stay quiet, cautiously shuffling his feet to avoid stepping on any dry branches or leaves. He was living an episode of *Mission: Impossible*, a favorite show of his grandfather's—not that inferior Tom Cruise dreck he wasn't permitted to view—though he did sneak a watch once and verified his grandfather's disdain. He would sit on the floor for hours in his grandparents' living room, watching TV spies at work.

Sliding forward from the protective cover of the trees, Ted crawled on his belly along the worn path until his ear was against the tent.

Quiet.

He lifted the canvas, stretching it until he could fit his head fully inside, then took one last glance behind him to ensure he hadn't attracted company. "Sam...Sam," he whispered. Her head hung awkwardly, the weight of her limp body straining against the ropes that were holding her upright.

138

Ted jumped to his feet and frantically began working to free Sam of her restraints. Pulling and tugging, the awareness of his surroundings diminished, and one tug-too-hard sent a crate crashing to the ground. He took one step to the left, and that was as far as he got before he was face-to-musty-hairy-chest with a nightmare of a beast. Sam roused in the corner of his eye—the final image before his world went black.

Sam let her body hang from the ropes which cut into her wrists and ankles. Keeping her eyes shut, she held in her screams of pain. The flap slapping against the doorway signaled she could move, as she heard the fading heaviness of Ted's body being dragged away.

Though he had been unable to remove the ropes, Ted had loosened them just enough. It gave Sam enough space between her hands to singe the cord and break free.

She searched the Ijiraq camp for signs of others, especially Maddie.

No, Maddie must have made it back, or else Ted wouldn't have made the boneheaded move of trying to rescue her on his own. The only voices in her head were those of the enemy: those who torture and kill and steal, who suck the life force from their victims so they can languish in this world for eternity.

The lesson of their persecution and emigration from their homeland was a fleeting memory, and only a few elders remained—the Dene among them—who had lived through the Dark Period, when many Ijiraq perished from starvation. The majority had been born on Earth and never truly understood the abuse their ancestors endured. No— they had only known aggression, never victimization. The Dene ensured his people would never feel persecution ever again, and every move was to guarantee their survival . . . at any cost.

Sam could feel the footsteps growing louder in her mind, along with the grumbling, psychotic rants of Nagha's internal dialog. She was free and had her powers, but there wasn't time to wade through the myriad voices from outside; she needed to escape before she was discovered.

Sam was making her way through the trees and away from the camp when a horn echoed throughout the mountains and valley. Nagha's voice followed in its wake, "We're coming for you!" A deafening bleat followed—a battle cry which riled the whole of the Ijiraq and swarmed Sam's head, momentarily dropping her to her knees.

War was coming. Sam had to find Puck and warn the Tahltan—her people. The time had come to lead, as Dene Tsesk'iye, the Raven Chief, and deliver them from this evil which had afflicted them for so many years. A wave of arrogant confidence consumed Sam as she transmitted to the entirety of the Ijiraq Nation: *We are mighty Tahltan warriors. You will know only the pain and suffering you have caused, returned to you sevenfold. You shall be defeated, never to plague this land again!*

CHAPTER TWELVE

Four days passed. The attack never came, and Ted was still gone. Sam assumed he was dead.

Daniel had left—against the council's pleas—to find and rescue Ted upon Sam's return, but it was no use. He had just been through hell, having thought he'd lost Ted and Maddie, only for both to be alive and safe, then plunged into the depths of despair once again. Daniel was on a mission which no one could stop, not even Sam.

Sam lay in bed, finally passed out from a combination of training, anxiety, and lack of sleep. Her people were mobilized and ready to fight—every weapon they could muster had been gathered, every weakness in their defenses plugged. It wouldn't matter which direction the Ijiraq came from; the Tahltan were prepared.

Sam yielded to Rose and the council, though her input was critical to their preparations based on her knowledge of the encampment and the sheer numbers of enemy combatants.

For the most part, Sam had spent the previous ninety-six hours training with Rose. Her powers were dangerous and she struggled to control them, especially when her emotions ran high. Rose had to constantly remind herself that, despite Sam's strength, courage, and maturity, she was still a child-leader who needed guidance and mentoring. If allowed, the bullheaded girl would run directly into the heart of enemy forces, wild and unhinged.

Under escort of the Number Two Lieutenant—an extra set of watchful eyes for added protection—Rose and Sam had ventured well into the woods, farther down river, out of view from the tribe, and out of sight of the Ijiraq.

"Keep calm, child. Control your emotions, and you'll control your powers." Sam would invariably break her concentration, favoring anger and plans to exterminate the vicious creatures. Rose kept repeating the same words.

After hearing some variation of Nana's mantra for the umpteenth time, Sam slumped to the ground in frustration. "I'm not going to be ready. They could attack any time now. What happens then?"

"You're putting an awful lot of pressure on yourself, dear. You are not, and never will be, the be-all-end-all for our people. It's not your job to save everyone. You must lead by example. Show strength and courage, always. This is not your fight alone, but all of ours. It is in this way that you are destined to save the Tahltan."

Sam's obstinance was in full force. "I will not let

142

another person die because of my inability to save them. This is my responsibility!"

She wasn't getting it. Rose turned away and dropped her head, mumbling something unintelligible. "She'll never learn." Sam heard that part clearly.

"Who are you talking to?"

"My daughter . . . even a sage old woman as myself still needs advice, at times."

"I'm your granddaughter. Not your daughter. Are you okay?" Sam was genuinely worried about Nana's mental state.

Rose turned back to Sam. "No, Sam, I am speaking to my daughter—your mother." Sam was stunned. "That's right. I can speak with her too."

"But . . . Can you see her, also?"

"No, though to see her again would be . . ." A catch in her throat stopped Rose from finishing.

Sam pulled herself off the ground and wrapped her arms around the tiny woman, her selfish pity party waning in favor of comforting her grandmother. "I wish you could. I did, but only once."

"I'm not sure that's possible, except in our dreams. Had you been dreaming?"

"No, Mom came to me when I was at the Ijiraq camp, but she disappeared quickly. I think she was trying to help keep me calm. I was so scared."

Rose pulled herself from Sam's embrace, placing a hand

on each of her granddaughter's shoulders, and said, "I wish to the stars that what you saw was Nan, but I'm not so sure."

Sam immediately grew agitated. "You don't believe me? I saw her with my own two eyes." She pulled away.

"The Ijiraq are tricksters, shape-shifters who will prey on your wishes and desires. I believe what you saw was a ruse."

"Why on Earth would they make themselves look like her? How would they even know what she looked like? I'm telling you, Nana, it was Mom." Sam was adamant.

"Dear, they can read your thoughts, but only when you are dreaming. They invade your mind like a leech and then use it against you to weaken your resolve. Did this happen after you had been knocked out? Had you been dreaming?"

Sam nodded, still wanting to believe it was her mother.

"We should get back to training," Rose said, though Sam wasn't satisfied with the explanation. "Lieutenant, please leave us. We will be okay. I need you to send for Puck and relay that we need him here at once. Please express to him that it's dire."

"Yes, Mother Rose." The young man left them.

"Mother Rose?" Sam asked.

Nana chuckled in her usual way to herself. "Those warrior-types. Always so courteous and proper. In due time you'll be Mother Sam." Rose roared with laughter. Sam couldn't help but join in.

The late afternoon sun was falling fast, along with the temperatures, but Rose pushed Sam through every exercise she could imagine. Sam was spent when Puck came hopping toward them from out of nowhere—the first anyone had seen of him since Sam's harrowing rescue of Maddie.

"Puck, where have you been?" Rose scolded. "We have requested your presence repeatedly. The Ijiraq will attack any moment now. We need your assistance."

Puck is sorry. Was scared after leaving Sam with Nagha. Puck is ashamed of his behavior. I failed you, Dene Tsesk'iye. You too, Dene Rose.

Rose responded with her mind, *There's no time for this, Deyo. Apologize with your actions, not your words.*

"Deyo?" Sam said. "I heard Nagha call you that when you were drawing the guards from the tent." Sam looked to Rose for an answer, but instead of relaying the story she had shared days earlier with the residents of Telegraph Creek, Rose turned to Puck and waved her hands over him. Sparks jumped from her fingers and a shower of embers fell over the little otter as she uttered words reminiscent of the language of the Ijiraq.

"I free you of your bonds, Puck. With this comes your loyalty to the tribe. You are no longer a servant of the Ijiraq or an emissary of the Tahltan. You are once again, Deyo, and I dub you a Tahltan warrior."

Thank you, Dene, responded the creature.

"I don't understand. What . . . who is Deyo?" Sam wanted to know.

With a nod from Rose, the small mammal began to twitch and contort in ways that frightened Sam. Before long, a beast arose standing eight feet tall with a rack of gnarled, razor-sharp horns extended another five feet. Piercing red slits for eyes glowed deep within its skull, and the grinning sideways maw was enough to send Sam flailing onto her back, a giant ball of fire cocked and ready for release.

"Stand down, Sam!" Rose yelled, but it was too late.

Sam launched the blazing red fireball directly at the monster's head, who ducked just in time, leaving only a slight singe on the points of its massive rack.

"Sam, stop! That is Puck! Puck is Deyo!"

Before he could stand and dust himself off, Deyo shifted back into the familiar form Sam had come to know — a smaller target and enough to get her to cease her fearful behavior. *Dene, it's me, Puck. I am Deyo. My given name.*

Sam was wide-eyed, attempting to make sense of things, but another ball of fire was building in her hands, just in case. "Deyo . . . You're one of them? An Ijiraq?" Sam was equally shocked, angry, and still frightened.

Please, Dene. Allow Puck to become Deyo. I'm your friend, please. No reason for the fright.

Rose gave Sam an approving nod—assuring her they would be safe. The fireball began to dissipate as Sam warily lowered her defenses, though not wholly.

Puck once again transformed into the towering beast. Before Sam could ask any more questions or attack out of fearful ignorance, Rose explained Deyo's story: who he was and how he had come to be Puck.

"I think I preferred you when you were cute and fuzzy," Sam said with no intention of humor. Rose chuckled anyway.

Deyo spoke as an Ijiraq for the first time in eighty years. His voice boomed deep, similar to Nagha in tone, resurrecting Sam's fright. "Permit me to reintroduce myself. I am Deyo, son of Kazune, Chief of the Ijiraq and architect of The Great Peace." The voice was captivating; eloquent, even.

"Your voice," Sam said.

"Puck was not granted the ability to speak as an otter. It is only through our abilities that he was able to communicate," explained Rose. "His vocabulary was that of the animal he represented. Simple and meek."

"I am here to serve you, Dene Tsesk'iye. I pledge my loyalty to the Tahltan; to you." He knelt before her. "For the past eighty years, the Ijiraq have treated me like an outcast. Even my own father refuses to see me as anything but a nuisance. Yet, Rose and the council have never treated me with anything but respect. For that, I offer myself."

"What will the others think?" Sam asked Rose.

Deyo answered for Rose. Sam watched as he shifted and transformed into an exceptional Tahltan villager, standing barely six feet tall, with jet black hair pulled back into a ponytail, stocky and all too familiar—it was Daniel! The likeness was so uncanny that Sam's initial interest in the shape-shifting process was lost to more pressing concerns.

"Puck . . . Sorry, I mean Deyo, won't that look a little odd if two Daniels are wandering around town?"

Deyo's face, as Daniel, turned dour.

"No. No, no, no," said Rose dropping to a knee. Sam rushed to her side and held her up by the elbow.

"What is it?" Sam looked to Deyo for the answer.

Sam's gut answered before Deyo could speak. "I'm sorry," said the Ijiraq, who had shifted back to his natural form. "It is another reason I remained hidden these past few days. I witnessed Daniel entering the camp in search of Ted. He didn't try to hide, nor did he make any attempt at diplomacy. Nagha's crew dispatched with him on sight. They were quite brutal. I'm sorry. I apologize for my candor."

Rose was doubled over, grabbing at her stomach, in physical pain at what she was hearing. Sam speculated whether Deyo's apology was for his candor or the bitter news he had to relive—he was still an Ijiraq, after all. A faucet of tears flowed from their eyes, including Deyo. Perhaps he was sincere in his apology.

The one-time otter had been helpless. Sam wondered if Deyo had been in Ijiraq form, if he might have been able to

148

stop them, if Daniel might still be alive.

"There was nothing you could have done, dear boy," said Rose, reading his thoughts.

"What about Ted? Is he okay?" a frantic Sam asked.

"I can't say for certain. Ted was being prepped for the ritual when Daniel showed up. I couldn't bear to watch as they drained Daniel's life force. I ran like a coward. I have to assume the worst." Sam wouldn't let herself believe Ted was gone.

Sam and Deyo helped Nana Rose to her feet, steadying her on each side as they walked back toward the village. They had agreed that Deyo should pose as Daniel for the time being, though it was a wretched thing for Rose to endure.

As they reached town, Rose directed Deyo toward Daniel's home with a stark warning to go straight to bed, for fear Maddie would catch on that the man who appeared to be Dad was merely an impostor. Sam escorted Rose to her house before going to her room.

"We have much to discuss tomorrow. An attack is still imminent, and we must train harder than ever. With Deyo on our side, we have plans to make, as well." With that, Rose bid Sam goodnight with a loving hug that was more for her own comfort than anything else.

"Goodnight, Nana."

As Sam reached her room, Jack met her in the hallway. She was in no mood to talk. "Can we catch up tomorrow, Dad?"

"Oh, okay, Princess. I was just hoping to find out how your training is going." Jack could see the salty stains on her cheeks. "Are you okay? You look like you've been crying."

"I'm just exhausted," she lied. "The training is harder than I expected."

"Get some rest, and we'll talk in the morning. Maybe get breakfast together?"

"Sure thing, Dad."

Jack reached out and hugged his little girl. She was growing up way too fast, and now she was expected to lead an entire band of people in a dangerous war for their very existence. It was a lot for Jack to process, let alone a fourteen-year-old. He squeezed her tight, and Sam had to pat him on the back to let him know to ease up and let go.

"Goodnight, Dad. I love you."

The entire village woke up at once the following day, when screams pierced the air from all corners of Telegraph Creek and beyond. Tribal members poured into the center of town, frantic as voices overlapped, calling out names . . . the names of their children.

The council gathered quickly to assess the situation: the entire population of Telegraph Creek children had gone missing. The Ijiraq had attacked, but not in the way they

had expected.

"Everybody! Please return to your homes and prepare yourselves!" Rose said in an amplified voice far more prominent than her stature. "Council is to convene immediately. Jack and Sam, please join us. Daniel, you too."

In his haste to discover the commotion, Jack hadn't noticed that Sam was not in their presence. "Rose!" Jack yelled over the din of distraught parents dispersing back to their homes. "Sam's not here. I think they took her."

"Maddie's gone, too," said Deyo, as Daniel and Rose waved them toward the council chambers.

As the doors shut, too many voices began speaking simultaneously, and Rose struggled to control them. Deyo provided the attention needed to quiet the room, transforming back into his natural form. The entire room was stunned by what they were witnessing.

Rose moved in front of Deyo. "Do I have your attention now?"

"You let one of them in here?" asked the youngest councilmember, grabbing for anything he could use as a weapon.

"Everyone, stand down," demanded Rose. "Council, I think you know our good friend here." Deyo shifted again — into Puck, then again, back to an Ijiraq.

Lee Ezerza was beside himself. "I thought my father took away his ability to shift?" he said, stunned.

"He did, but Deyo stands with us now. As assurance

for his loyalties to the tribe, I restored his ability to practice his magic. Does anyone have a problem with that?"

Heads shook throughout the room.

"Wait, where is Daniel?" Jack astutely asked. Deyo transformed into the man Jack recognized.

"Daniel . . . the real Daniel, is gone," Rose said, breaking the news of the heroic yet tragic actions he had undertaken to save his son. "We will mourn Daniel in due time, but first, we must get our children back."

"And we must avenge Daniel's death!" said another councilperson.

Rose was adamant in her stance. "We are not a vengeful people. The Tahltan fight only to defend our freedom and our right to live peacefully on our lands. We do not seek blood for blood. Do I make myself clear?"

The entire council nodded in agreement. The councilperson who had demanded vengeance offered plentiful apologies to Rose.

"What do we need to do?" asked Jack. "Tell us how we get the kids back."

"We don't . . . yet," said Deyo. The Ijiraq was bold in his assertion to the group.

"Rose?" said Lee Ezerza.

Rose had been conversing telepathically with Deyo while the others bickered among themselves. They had a plan. "Deyo will be my right hand in this endeavor. What he says goes, no questions asked. Please sit and listen."

The council took their seats and listened intently to the plan Deyo laid before them. Not one of them questioned it; they were united.

CHAPTER THIRTEEN

S am instinctively reached for her throbbing head and nearly pulled her shoulder from its socket. Her hands were bound behind her . . . again. But this time, cold steel enveloped her hands and wrists. She attempted to open her eyes, but only blackness remained. Her eyes had been taped shut, her hands and wrists bound in an iron chamber behind her back.

She was back in captivity and could hear the hoots and hollers of the monsters outside. Sam screamed out as the voices—the voices of scores of children—flooded her head, the outburst muffled by the cloth gag stuffed so far down her throat she could barely breathe, and the cries of those kids rang through her head.

Sam remembered nothing. She had been asleep in her bed after an exhausting day of training and having just learned Puck's true identity . . . now, here, back in the Ijiraqs' den, a prisoner with all of the other Tahltan children. *This has to be a bad dream.* Sam willed herself to awaken, but it

didn't take long to realize this was her reality. She screamed again, as loud as she could, hoping to attract the attention of someone—anyone.

She got her wish: the distinct sound of the canvas tent flap slapped closed against itself. Whoever it was stayed silent except for meek footsteps lightly crunching the earth, moving closer. She could smell the creature—wet matted hair mixed with pine and the sharp iron bite of fresh blood—it filled her senses. She attempted to read its mind but only heard a child's voice, then the cacophony of Ijiraq tongues, a swarm which drowned out everything else, even the whimpers and cries of the Tahltan kids.

The cloth gag wasn't even fully pulled from her mouth when she spoke. "Who's there? What's going on? Leave my people alone and sacrifice me. I'm all you need. Please!" The rapid-fire slurry of questions and pleas went unanswered. "Ouch!" Sam yelled as the tape was ripped from her eyes; she was pretty sure, along with half of her eyebrows and lashes.

"Shh, no talking," said a tender voice.

Sam was still adjusting to the flood of light, wishing her hands were free to rub her blurry vision into focus. The only thing clear was the silhouette of an undersized— though still almost six foot tall—Ijiraq, whose horns were rounded and barely three feet across. A juvenile, or so Sam believed. But why was it in here? What business did it have with her?

Sam's eyes cleared, but her right eye was still a bit cloudy. The creature standing before her was slight of build, its still fuzzy rack confirming Sam's notion of the relative youth of the animal. Though not threatening, it was an Ijiraq, and Sam let her eyes begin to burn a deep sapphire. Inside her iron cuffs, sparks jumped and occasionally found an outlet through a seam in the metal—the contained energy providing a painful shock which Sam endured, choosing to show her audience the potential of her power, despite her discomfort.

The slender Ijiraq child slowly backed up and cowered, raising its arms in front of its face and covering its ruby eyes, an act of self-preservation in fear of the powerful prisoner it was assigned to. "That's right, you should be scared. You should all be very scared of what I will do to you once I am free." The young Ijiraq turned to exit the tent, but Sam still wanted answers. "No, stop. Please come back." She lowered her guard, allowing her eyes to return to their natural blue. The Ijiraq turned back and shook its head, still intent on getting far away from the threatening girl. "Please," Sam repeated.

The child stopped, tilting its head sideways as if waiting for more, waiting for the girl with the glowing eyes to give it a reason to stick around. It remained silent, and Sam was uncertain whether this coy display was for show or a language barrier she had to overcome. Perhaps both.

"Can you understand me?" she asked. The creature

156

nodded and moved closer. "What's your name? My name is Sam."

Putting a hand to its chest, the Ijiraq responded, "Behgehyalé." The voice was soft and feminine, though Sam wasn't sure if Ijiraq followed traditional human gender norms.

"Behgehyalé. That's a pretty name. It's a mouthful but beautiful. What does it mean?"

"Behgehyalé," she repeated, followed by what Sam assumed was an explanation of the name, though she didn't understand.

"May I call you Yalé, for short?" The creature nodded. "Yalé, I'm sorry, but I don't understand." Sam transmitted a message to Behgehyalé in hopes of breaking the language barrier: *Show me with your mind. Show me what you said with pictures in your mind. Does that make sense?*

With an affirmative dip of her horns, Yalé closed her eyes and concentrated, forming a picture in her mind. What materialized was the most beautiful black and blue butterfly with bright yellow spots which resembled eyes. Sam couldn't help but smile, and it put them both at ease.

"Butterfly," said Sam, and Yalé's eyes brightened to an almost pinkish hue. A smile—creepy and sideways, but a smile nonetheless—crossed the creature's long face. *How old are you, little butterfly?* The number forty-six came into focus. *But you're just a kid. Like me.*

Sam recalled Nana Rose's stories from her training,

how Ijiraq were immortal so long as they could keep stealing the life force of tribal children. But even without immortality, Ijiraq could live for over three hundred years. Sam believed Behgehyalé to be more or less the same age as her. That and her friendly demeanor meant Sam had a potential ally on the inside, someone she could use to her advantage, to stop the slaughter of her people.

Do you know Deyo? Sam asked. An image of her friend formed—an image of Puck, playing with an even younger version of the girl. They were playing hide-and-seek in the forest, near the river. Puck was cheating by hiding in the water, but she still found him.

Tears welled in the Ijiraq's eyes. "Deyo, brother." She clearly knew a few words.

Sam was incredulous. "Puck . . . I mean, Deyo, is your brother?"

"Brother," Behgehyalé repeated.

"If you let me go, I can take you to him. I know where he is," Sam said.

Yalé shook off Sam's offer and was once again attempted to exit. Perhaps she was fearful of her clan, of the trouble it would bring if she released their most prized prisoner. Maybe the thought of seeing her brother was too much. Sam couldn't read her any longer; she had shut Sam out of her mind—it was an ability that startled her. She transmitted to Yalé, begging for her help, but it was either ignored or not getting through.

The Ijiraq approached Sam and gagged her again, though not as forcefully or as deep as previously. Sam's eyes began to glow again in hopes that the girl would stop, but it didn't work, and the tape blinded her once again.

"Hey, who's in there?" said Nagha, barging in. "Behgehyalé, what are you doing? You don't belong here." The young one cowered, expecting a beating that never came. "Get out of here now. Your father wants to see you. Go to Dene, at once!" Behgehyalé scampered out of the tent, but not before Sam transmitted one last plea for help and a promise to see her brother. "Finally awake, huh?" said Nagha. "You gonna be a good little princess, or do I need to turn off the lights again?"

Sam thrashed back and forth, forcefully attempting to loosen her bindings. A muffled fit of rage pushed through the cloth stuffed in her mouth.

"Have it your way, Princess," Nagha said, as Sam's already dark world went darker with another crack across the back of her skull.

When Sam awoke again, she was lying on the cold ground. It proved a sudden shock that sent her scrambling backward on her hands and knees to the back of the tent, a fireball at the ready. Yalé stood across from her with a welcoming message—a picture of her hugging her brother in her thoughts.

The fireball dissipated at once.

"You changed your mind. But, why?" Sam asked.

Yalé showed Sam a horrific scene: the children of the Tahltan being marched into the center of the Ijiraq village and lined up, all blindfolded and bound by rope. They stood before a fire where one at a time, the kids were sacrificed. Their auras. Their souls. Their life force slipping from their persons, encircling the Ijiraq tribe, then collected in a large vessel, a vessel being held by the Ijiraq Dene, Behgehyalé's father. Deyo's father. The bodies slumped over — dead.

Sam couldn't take it anymore. "Stop! No more! Please, stop!" Sam pried herself from the gruesome scene in Yalé's head. "This already happened?" Sam was choking back sobs.

"No." The simple reply was a relief, but it didn't change that this was coming if she didn't act fast. Outside of her own escape, she had no plan that would save the other children. "Watch," Behgehyalé requested, pointing to her mind.

Sam was hesitant to watch any more imminent carnage; even if it wasn't real, it would be soon enough. She gave in, though, as the youngster insisted, continually pointing to her head.

The next image Sam saw was her mother. It was a scene she'd played in her head a thousand times since Nan's death: The last Bigfoot trip they had taken as a family, gathered around a campfire making S'mores, laughing

without a care in the world. It was the most enduring memory she had of her mom . . . of them as a family.

"But, how did you . . ." Sam had spent an inordinate amount of time unconscious in this tent, and she remembered the Ijiraq's ability to invade a person's dreams while they slept. Yalé had been in her head. It was invasive and disturbing.

Sam chose to keep her emotions in check this time. Yalé was trying to show her something, something important.

Yalé opened her mind to Sam and said, "Watch."

Sam wasn't ready for what she witnessed next. The young Ijiraq began to transform. The transformation wasn't so off-putting, having watched Deyo perform the act days earlier—how long had she been here? It was who Yalé became which daggered her heart. "Mom?"

She knew it was not her mother, but seeing her likeness, knowing it wasn't a dream, and standing right in front of her . . . Sam ran to the doppelganger and hugged her tight. The feel. Even her smell. It was her mom, but it wasn't. She lost herself in the moment, despite the truth behind the replication. Yalé could feel Sam's pain and her joy, and hugged her back.

Sam reluctantly stepped back. "Why are you showing me this? Why my mom?" Sam said, wiping tears.

Yalé pointed at Sam.

"Me? I don't understand what you want. Show me."

Yalé transformed back to her natural state, then back to Nan, then into Deyo, and then into Nagha. The last one scared Sam before Yalé returned back to her own form. She once again pointed to Sam.

"You want *me* to shift?" Sam asked, and Yalé nodded enthusiastically. "I don't know how to do that."

The creature pointed to her head once again, instructing Sam to watch. Yalé showed Sam a vision of herself shifting into the form of an Ijiraq—of Yalé—and Yalé transforming into Sam. It was clear now what she was suggesting: A *Freaky Friday*-like body swap that would allow Sam to escape and get help; Yalé willing to take Sam's place for a chance to see her brother once again.

"That's a brilliant plan, but like I said, I can't shift. I don't know that magic, only . . ." Sam conjured a ball of fiery energy.

"Try. Think. Be," Yalé requested. Sam was starting to think the Ijiraq knew quite a bit more English than she was letting on, but she didn't question it.

Sam was skeptical, but the plan was too perfect not to try. She closed her eyes and imagined herself transforming into her beastly friend. If she could see it, her face was contorting and grimacing and would have been amusing in a different situation.

Nothing happened. Sam tried again and again, without success. "It's no use. I can't do it."

Yalé pointed to her head, another "movie" ready for

Sam to watch. This time it started with a flash which subsided to an image of Ash. The phoenix was helping Sam with her fledgling powers. The fire and energy jumping from her fingertips—a revelation.

"My powers . . . they came from Ash? I control fire like Ash!" Sam had indeed borrowed—nay, pulled from—the magic which Ash had bestowed upon her. Her magic was his magic. That meant, "I can shift?"

"Use heart. Try. Think. Be," Yalé repeated.

Sam once again concentrated, feeling the Ijiraq's magic, pulling it from the creature while imagining herself shapeshifting into the form of the deadly monster, becoming a vision of her enemy. She opened her eyes, disappointed yet again.

"It's no use, Yalé. That's not my magic; it's yours."

"Look," said Yalé, pointing at Sam.

Sam looked down in astonishment. She was covered in dark brown fur, and hooves had taken the place of her hands. She reached up and could feel the rack of horns on her head; they felt strong, unbreakable. She had shifted. She had become an Ijiraq. Yalé shifted, and Sam was staring at her own likeness.

The wondrous moment was short-lived with the clock ticking. Sam bound Yalé to the tent, complete with gag and tape over her eyes, and installed the iron cuffs. She was a captive once again . . . but she wasn't.

She transmitted to Yalé, "Thank you, friend. I will

return to set you and the others free. And I will bring your brother to you, as promised." Sam confidently walked out of the tent and into a crowd of Ijiraq villagers. Not one of them looked her way—she was one of them.

Sam's ability to absorb the magic of mythical creatures was beyond her imagination. Was this what Nana meant about the unlimited potential of her powers? Could she swim like a mermaid? Fly like a Pegasus? Was she alluring and powerful like the Fae? Wait, was she Fae? The possibilities were endless, though the time for exploration would need to wait.

CHAPTER FOURTEEN

Telegraph Creek was home to only four hundred Tahltan, but the children numbered more than one hundred—one-hundred-plus of their beloved children, stolen during the night to be used for sacrifice so a savage race of beasts could live on in immortality.

The village seemed desolate; the lack of laughing and screaming children turned the once-thriving community into an eerily haunted ghost town. The adults refused to come out of their homes, barricaded inside against a possible attack that could wipe them out . . . that was until Deyo and Rose were ready to unveil their plan.

At the center of the town square, Lee Ezerza clanged an old brass bell repeatedly, notifying the masses to gather around the dais—he didn't stop until all of the villagers were present.

Rose shushed the crowd. "Everybody, gather around and listen carefully. We know how scared you are for the children and yourselves, but the time for action has arrived.

The future of our people is at stake, and we must, as our ancestors before us, take up arms to defeat an evil enemy intent on wiping us out. We have a responsibility to each other and the surrounding First Nations communities to eradicate the Ijiraq once and for all, so that no more harm can ever come to our tribes."

A voice boomed from the crowd, somewhat melancholy and matter of fact in his appeal. "Dene, if our ancestors couldn't defeat them and were forced to make an evil pact just to survive, what's to say we can defeat them? We are not the warriors our grandparents or their grandparents were. We have become complacent. Fighting is not our nature anymore. The past eighty years have made us weak."

"You have a legitimate concern, son," Rose continued. "I am proud of all of you. I am proud of what this tribe has achieved through peace over the last eighty years. War and violence should never be the answer. But today, we have to make a difficult choice of violating our beliefs and the fiber of who we are to save our young ones from certain death."

The tall man continued, "And how are we supposed to do this? Our military is not much more than a few deep, only here to protect us from intruders who never come."

In the form of Daniel, Deyo spoke up, "This will undoubtedly be dangerous, and we are asking for every able-bodied person to volunteer and join us in this fight. But we will not force you. It's your decision, and we will give our lives to save your kids, even if you choose to stay in the

safety of your homes. Please come forward if you wish to take up arms."

The voices began to grow as people discussed their choice. Some volunteered without hesitation, but some waited to see how strong the army would be. When all was said and done, their might grew to fifty strong. It was paltry compared to the number of Ijiraq they would face.

The questioning man from the crowd was not among them, though he spoke up once again. "I ask again, how do you expect this lot to take down those monsters?"

Deyo said, "Because they do not know what's coming." With that, Deyo transformed before their eyes from Daniel into Puck, then into his Ijiraq form. Screams emanated from the crowd, and even those who volunteered scattered from the dais in terror. Deyo let out a guttural roar that sent some scrambling from the square, but quieted them all.

"Deyo is one of us!" Rose insisted to the dispersed crowd. "I have granted him his original form so that he may help us in our fight. Deyo is our secret weapon, an insider they have not seen and whom they are not expecting. He is an Ijiraq in physical appearance only. He is a Tahltan in heart, mind, and spirit."

"He's a monster!" yelled a woman.

"That freak is one of them!" yelled another.

And another, "What did he do with Daniel?"

And another, "Child stealer!" A chorus of "child stealer" began to erupt from the villagers.

The crowd had found their fighting spirit and was merciless in their denial of Deyo. They were ready to attack, to string him up and make an example of him. They were out of control—near riotous.

A bright red light began to grow from the dais. Rose conjured an enormous ball of light which shimmered and expanded above the village square until it began to vibrate, finally reaching a crescendo and exploding. It temporarily blinded those who looked at it, but the effective crowd control measure got her people in line.

"Do I have your attention, now?" Rose snapped. "Daniel was captured trying to save Ted," she lied, not wanting to ignite tensions any further. "Besides, where was that passion when we asked you to join us, to save your children? You will all respect and obey Deyo. He is your brother now. He is also our leader on this quest, and it is he who will bring our children home. So I will ask once again, who is with us? Take your place by our sides."

The villagers started to amass, once again. This time their numbers grew to seventy-three. The tall, skeptical man still remained on the sideline. "Join us, brother," insisted Deyo.

"I refuse to fight alongside such an evil creature, as yourself."

"Your choice will be respected, and I will still give my life if it means bringing home your daughter," Deyo said.

Tall Man scoffed and returned to his home.

Once dusk set in, Deyo—leading a fully-armed militia of Tahltan parents hell-bent on retrieving their abducted children—marched silently upriver through the Stikine Valley, where they could flank the Ijiraq encampment with hopes of catching them by surprise. They did not use any lanterns or lights of any kind, ensuring their presence wasn't discovered any earlier than preferred.

They reached the backside of the village and it was pitch black, though the bonfire at the center of the makeshift town blazed like a furnace, warming their faces nearly 200 yards away. They hid in the trees, behind the tents on both sides of the main thoroughfare. Ijiraq were bustling about in preparation for the coming ritual sacrifice, too busy to notice they were being surrounded.

Deyo held his forces, instructing them to stay in place. He had given them a warning before leaving Telegraph Creek: "You will see your children, and you will want to run for them. You will want to take your vengeance, but this mission will fail if you act on those feelings. We must be calculated, calm of mind, exacting in our execution if we are to be victorious and set our people free." It was a tall ask for untrained soldiers—civilians—who were emotionally invested in the mission, and one, he knew, put them at a disadvantage.

As they sat and waited, Deyo and Jack scanned the camp. "The kids must be in the tents," said Jack. "If we move now, the kids should be out of harm's way from any fighting."

"Patience, friend. It is still a risky proposition. They have the numbers, and our people are not the most adept with the weapons they've been given."

"Perhaps, we shouldn't be attacking a superior foe," Jack surmised.

"Perhaps diplomacy can still be attained," Deyo shot back.

"I thought we came here to get the kids back by any means necessary—by force."

"Violence is still a last resort, but if it is to happen, it will be tonight. We had no choice but to be prepared for it." Deyo had more to say but got redirected by a young Ijiraq running across the top of the ridge opposite camp. He recognized her immediately. "Behgehyale?" he said to himself.

"I'm sorry, what was that?" Jack asked.

"The girl. There, on the ridge. It's my sister, Behgehyale. What is she doing?"

"She looks like she's running away," said Jack.

"I agree, but why? If she is not here during the sacrifice, she will not absorb the life force. She will not remain immortal."

"I thought that's what we wanted, Deyo." Jack was

confused, and thoughts of Deyo's loyalty started to waffle in his mind. Had he just tricked the tribe into coming here? Did they just walk right into a trap—more souls to feed their lust for immortality? "Deyo, what's going on? You're making me nervous."

"I feel your hesitation, Jack, your questioning. The Tahltan are my people, and I will not betray them. But she is still my sister, and she's in trouble. She's trying to escape for a reason, and I need to find out. Stay here, and that's an order."

With the wave of a hoof, Deyo gave a silent order for everyone to continue holding their positions, then made his way between the tents and into the center of the village. It had been eighty years since he'd stepped in front of his kin as an Ijiraq. Most knew him only as Puck. He headed for the ridge, for his sister. A straight line was the quickest way, and she was already nearly out of sight.

"You, where are you going?" asked Nagha, stopping Deyo as he headed up the hill to the ridgeline. He turned cautiously, but Nagha did not recognize him.

"Dene asked me to fetch Puck," he lied.

"What does Dene want with that cowardly rat?" Nagha said.

"He didn't say. I didn't ask." Deyo responded.

"Very well, be gone, but make it quick. There's a lot to do before the ritual begins, and we still need to gather supplies for the attack."

The attack? They still planned on attacking, even after killing the children in cold blood. Deyo did his best to keep his composure. "Yes, Nagha, I understand and will return promptly." Had Deyo known of the attack, he might not have waited on diplomacy.

He continued up the ridge into the thicket of trees to track down his sister, finally catching up near the closest *inuksuk* to the camp. "Behgehyale!" The girl kept moving. "Behgehyale! Stop!" But she continued unabated. "Get back here, Behgehyale! I am your brother, and you will do as I say!"

The young Ijiraq came to a sliding stop.

Deyo approached his sister for the first time as an Ijiraq. She had been born after his banishment and transformation into Puck. "Deyo?" she asked softly. "Is that really you?"

"Yes, sister."

"Deyo, before this goes any further, I need to show you something." Behgehyale began to shift, and Sam appeared, standing before her Ijiraq friend.

"Sam? Why are you showing me Sam? You saw her? Where is she?" Deyo stammered.

"Deyo, slow down. It's me. I am Sam."

"But . . . you shifted. How?" he asked.

"Yalé. She taught me," said Sam.

"Yalé?"

"I call her that for short," Sam replied with a slight

giggle. "She freed me and showed me that I can shift too. It was her plan that allowed me to escape."

Deyo surmised his sister's whereabouts. "So that means she's . . . "

"Yes, she looks like me and is tied up in the second to last tent. She agreed to this if I would bring you to her. I was on my way back to tell you and Nana. Things are about to get really ugly down there."

"I know. We're assembled on the backside of the camp; seventy-five of us, including your dad. We were biding our time for the right moment to attack and free all of you kids. Though I still have one last resort I'd like to try, to avoid bloodshed."

"Then let's go. From what I can tell—from what Yalé told me—the sacrifices are going to begin in the next couple hours."

"I ran into Nagha when I came to chase you down. He didn't recognize me, but I could tell they were getting close. I told him that Dene asked me to call on Puck."

"Then let's give them what they're expecting," and Sam turned into the little otter. *Lead the way,* she transmitted with a squeak.

The odd pair reached the top of the ridge and looked down in horror. The children were led from the tents and lined up fronting the fire, the image exactly what Yalé had shown Sam earlier.

What are we going to do? asked Sam. *Why are they*

starting so early?

"Calm, Sam. This is the cleansing ritual. The Ijiraq cannot consume a spirit they deem to be dirty. This will take a while, especially with so many to perform."

His words weren't reassuring, given the scene playing out in front of her.

"Let's go. Act dumb and clumsy, like Puck. I will do the rest," said Deyo.

The two made their way down the hill, Sam purposely falling head-over-tail as she'd seen Puck do in the past. When she righted herself, she was at the feet of the Dene. He was far more imposing than the others, despite his hunched posture. His gnarl of horns was worn down and cracking, his fur was a mix of white and brown, his eyes a shade of red nearing black—he was ancient. Certainly older than three hundred years. Sam assumed well over a thousand.

"What do you want, Puck?" Dene Kazune asked, annoyed.

Sam was afraid to respond, fearful of giving up her identity.

"I don't have time for these games, son. Say what you need to say, or be gone!"

Nagha approached, immediately eyeing Deyo. "That was quick. Dumb otter must have been close, huh?" he said with a cackle.

"What's this about?" demanded the Chief.

"I was told you wanted to see Puck, Dene," replied

174

Nagha. "At least that's what he said," pointing to Deyo.

"Nonsense, I have no need for this traitorous filth, especially right now!"

Nagha realized the ruse and called out the Ijiraq for his deception. "Why would you lie to me and bring this vermin here?"

Deyo responded, "Because I needed to see my father. I needed to appeal to his sense of tradition and ask that he hold up his end of the contract."

"Your father isn't here, boy. Get back in line with the others and get ready for the ceremony," Nagha demanded.

The old man lifted his head as high as his hunchback would allow. "Deyo? Is that really you?" He doubted whether the Ijiraq standing in front of him was his son, especially in the presence of Puck.

Deyo nodded. "Yes, father. You need to stop this massacre at once. This is not who we are."

He chose to ignore the feeling. "You are not 'we'; you are a simpleton, a furry rodent who lives in the dirty waters of the Stikine," he said pointing at Puck. "And you are an imposter! Get them out of my sight now, Nagha."

Before they could be escorted away, Sam shifted back into Yalé. "Dad!" yelled the Ijiraq girl. "This is your son. This is Deyo. Do it," she said to Deyo, and he transformed into Puck.

"How is this possible?" Dene asked incredulously.

"Deyo shifted back to his natural state and answered,

"I made a deal with the Tahltan council. A deal for my freedom, but it requires letting these children go home. Abiding by the treaty our peoples agreed to eighty years ago."

Dene Kazune now believed it *was* his son standing before him, though his request was asinine, at best. "Deyo. Always the traitor. Making new deals with our enemy for your own gain."

Deyo begged. "Father, please. This is a slaughter, not a ceremony. This isn't right. Rose offered herself to you as a tribute to ensure another eighty years of peace. She's willing to do this for her people and for the Ijiraq. Let the kids go."

The Dene paced back and forth, hobbling with his cane, taking serious consideration of the offer.

Nagha laughed, "You're a fool, Deyo! Always the fool!"

"Silence!" demanded Dene, turning to his son. "You tell Rose that the only deal will be for her precious granddaughter. If she agrees, the peace will remain. If not, then she'll see the end of her people by morning."

"No!" yelled Yalé. "No!"

"No? You question me, young one?"

Before their eyes, Yalé shifted and Sam stood before them. "I said no! You will not tell Rose anything. I give myself freely for my people."

"Sam, no!" Jack yelled from the tree line. "No!"

"Take the girl and prep her," said Dene Kazune to Nagha, who all too eagerly manhandled Sam, knocking her

176

around. "Deyo, you will take your people—the children and those you've brought with you—and you will leave us, never to return for another eighty years. If I so much as smell you near this camp before then, there will be no more peace, and I will eradicate the Tahltan, once and for all."

One last solemn plea from Deyo, "Can you please return her body to her people? To her father? She deserves a proper burial." The request was accepted with a nod from the Ijiraq chief.

Deyo and the other adults rounded up the children as fast as possible and made their way toward the ridge, allowing the *inuksuk* to guide them back to the village. Jack was in a state of shock that he would never see his daughter again. He couldn't move. Deyo had to carry him back on his shoulder.

They would have their peace and no one would have to die . . . except Sam.

CHAPTER FIFTEEN

The exodus back to Telegraph Creek was swift.

Deyo placed Jack in his room and Lee Ezerza administered a sedative to help the father rest without falling deeper into depression. It was impossible to process losing his daughter. Lee would stay with Jack while he slept. It was a band-aid, but the tribe would be there to help him through his mourning. The elation which permeated the village upon having the other children returned would have been too much for Jack to bear. Watching the other families reunite would have pushed him past the point of no return. *First Nan. Now Sam.*

"Dad! Dad!" Ted could be heard from every corner of town. Maddie tagged along as they searched for Daniel. "Dad!"

Rose and the Council had gathered in their chambers. They could hear the heart-wrenching calls from the boy, distracting them from the hotwash of the previous night's events. They couldn't hold onto the truth any longer. Rose

called on Daniel's children to join them.

As Ted and Maddie entered, the forlorn faces of the council members greeted them. The sight of Deyo was still unnerving and caused Maddie to move to Ted's side, grabbing his arm and hiding from the creature's direct stare.

"You wanted to see us?" asked Ted, keeping an untrusting eye on Deyo.

"Come in, dears," Rose said solemnly, walking to greet them. "I hear that you are looking for your father." Rose paused, tears welling. The kids knew the news they were about to receive and were crying before Rose could say another word. She simply said, "I'm sorry," and pulled them into an embrace, holding them from falling to the ground as they wailed in agony.

"This isn't possible," Maddie said, fighting the tug in her throat. "I just saw him the night before we were taken. This doesn't make any sense."

"Daniel ... your father left to retrieve Ted. He was captured ..." Rose didn't finish the sentence, sparing the children the details of his gruesome end.

Ted grew angry in his despair. "This is your fault!" he said to Deyo. "You ... your people did this!" He lunged at the hulking beast who dodged his swipes as he pushed back from the table—not that Ted, even in this rage, could have done any harm to him. The youngest council member grabbed Ted to hold him back for his own safety, not Deyo's.

"I apologize for the ruse, young one. What you saw

was me, as your father," said Deyo to Maddie. "I had to make it appear that your dad was still here, or it would have raised too many questions among the tribe and made saving Ted, and you, far more difficult."

"I'm going to kill you!" screamed Ted, trying to fight free. Ted's bravado was genuine; the hate and rage which filled him, all too real.

"No, Ted," replied Maddie, "this isn't his fault. It's Sam's. We were living in peace with the Ijiraq until she showed up. Good riddance. Now we can sleep again without worrying about another attack." Maddie excused herself from the chambers without another word, just the smug satisfaction that her rival was dead and she could take her rightful place as the next in line, Dene of her tribe. Losing her father had suddenly taken a backseat to her newfound sense of entitlement.

"Let go of me," said Ted, ripping himself from the councilman's grip. He turned his back to the council and walked toward the door. "I still blame you, filthy monster!" Deyo accepted the hatred. There would be no changing the boy's mind; his pain controlled him. The doors slammed behind him.

"I apologize to all of you. Perhaps it's best that I not be here," said Deyo.

Rose said, "There is nothing to apologize for. You've done nothing wrong, and we will need you if we are to make things right for our people. We need to get Sam back."

One of the council members spoke up, "But I thought the Ijiraq sacrificed her last night. We can send a contingent to retrieve the body. Jack deserves to have her back."

Deyo responded, "There's no need. The Dene assured me we would get her back when they were finished. If they had completed the ritual, she'd have been brought here immediately. The Ijiraq are afraid of death despite their appetite for taking lives. They would have rid themselves of the body, by fire or by following through with their promise. I have no reason to believe they'd renege."

"Then, what is the plan to get her back? Surely they will not waste any more time keeping her alive," said the councilman.

The council members looked at each other across the table, waiting for someone to offer a solution, but all remained silent.

Sam and Yalé darted through the trees, over rocks, and up the steep hillside on the far side of the Stikine River. They were soaked, having safely made it across the rapids, both in the form of Puck. They ran and ran and ran, constantly looking skyward, expecting the ravens with the red eyes to follow them and keep them from a successful escape. Anytime they spied a bird circling up high, they transformed into otters. It slowed their progress but provided some security from the army pursuing them.

The river would have been the quickest way back to the village, but it left them exposed to the sharp-eyed bird which could have spotted them, even if submerged. Instead, they chose a land route and hoped that the Ijiraq wouldn't think to look for them in the next valley over. They would continue parallel to the river and eventually back to Telegraph Creek.

"Yalé, slow down; we need to stop," said Sam. She wasn't as quick-footed or as lung-strong as her Ijiraq friend. They had been going nonstop for nearly five miles. Even when Sam went for a jog, it was never more than three miles, and certainly not at such a breakneck pace.

They were still two miles from their destination. Sam decided they should cross back over the river downstream from the town, near the area where Nana Rose had been training her—the water was calmer, and there was far more tree cover to aid in their attempt at clandestinely sliding back into the village.

"Over here," said Yalé. A large outcropping of rocks formed a small open-air cave that shielded them from an overhead view.

Sam was winded and still attempting to catch her breath when she said, "Thank you. I owe you everything. I literally owe you my life."

Hours earlier, a battered and bruised Sam—thanks to Nagha—had been tied to an upright log pole at the center of the Ijiraq camp. It was elevated by a six-foot mound of dirt and boulders which kept the heavy rail in place, even with the weight of a human hanging from it.

Sam never fought back, not once. No attempts to escape, no fireballs or energy, no sapphire eyes burning a hole in her captors. She had accepted her fate and knew that the Tahltan could once again live in peace through her sacrifice. She was ready to join her mom on the other side.

As punishment for her disobedience, for befriending Sam and setting her free, Behgehyale was forced to prep Sam for the ceremony. The cleansing ritual was customarily reserved for mid-level Ijiraq shamans who had been through at least some training. Any misstep in the cleansing could compromise the ability to capture their victim's life force. Yalé was supervised, given the extreme importance of this particular sacrifice.

Sam was bathed in a copper tub filled with mother's milk, lavender, and pine, then dressed in a stark white gossamer gown. Her hair was intricately braided: two even cords of hair intertwined and held in place above her head to resemble Ijiraq horns. An otherwise naive onlooker might have mistaken the primping and grooming as appropriate for a princess awaiting her coronation.

When the pampering concluded—the ritual within the ritual—Sam was led to the gallows, tied so tight by Nagha that her hands turned blue and fell numb. She couldn't muster a fireball even if she wanted to.

Sam lifted her head and Nagha stood before her. He slapped her across the face, and said, "Watch." The lone guard on duty laughed at the pain inflicted on the prisoner. Nagha turned to him, "Something funny?"

"No, sir," the guard replied.

"Then I suggest you pay less attention to me and do your job." The guard took his cue, turned his back, and continued his watch. Nagha turned his attention back to Sam, "Now watch!" he said, pointing to his head.

Sam watched a daring sequence of events where she and Yalé escaped and ended with the reunion Yalé desired with her brother, and Sam with Jack. Sam said, "Why are you showing me this? Why give me hope only to cut me down?" Nagha had been crueler at that moment than he had ever shown previously.

"Not Nagha. Yalé," said the false image of the beast in front of her.

Sam understood and appreciated Yalé's attempt to rescue her but was resigned to her fate. She transmitted, *No, Yalé, it's too late. Deyo will find you; I know he will. Let me go.*

Sam was right, it was too late, but Yalé's plan was already in action as she swiped a sharp blade across Sam's

wrists and fully through the bindings, just a hair's breadth from breaking her skin.

The guard turned at the sound of the ropes dropping to the ground. "Sir?"

"Mind your business. I'm not done with this one yet," said Yalé as Nagha, slapping Sam across the face once again.

Okay, can you ease up a bit; that really hurts.

A look of remorse mixed with embarrassment crossed Nagha's face. It was an odd expression to see, and not one anyone would ever expect on this particular face. It was almost comical.

No one paid any attention as Nagha escorted the prisoner past the row of tents, to the end of the thoroughfare and across the tree line. "Now, run!" Yalé instructed Sam.

Sam didn't have time to think; she ran as fast as she could, doing her best to keep up with Yalé. Five minutes had passed before anyone noticed, and then hoots and hollers of Ijiraq sentries scattered in all directions to retrieve their prey. Within a few minutes, ravens were circling above, though the fugitives were under a dense canopy that kept them well hidden.

The girls rested for a full hour before Sam was ready to push for home. *Home*—it was the first time she thought of Telegraph Creek in that way. She was expected to be their leader, which meant she *was* home. Seattle and Sedona had been mere stops on a journey to where she belonged.

Sam and Yalé scanned the skies, peaking from their hovel—all was clear. They started slow but soon found themselves once again running at full speed. It took only minutes to arrive at the river crossing.

Unlike where they had crossed before, the water here was glassy but twice as wide. They slipped into the icy river—chilly even for an otter—and made their way across. They hadn't made it halfway when a flock of red-eyed killers began to circle above, waiting for the right time to swoop down.

When they reached the far embankment, they remained in the water. *Stay here. I will take care of them. If they come for you, dive deep*, instructed Sam. Yalé agreed.

Sam turned back toward the center of the river and dove down nearly thirty feet. She cut through the water, then ascended as fast as she could toward the riverbank, propelling herself through the air. She landed on one knee and once again looked like Sam. A deep, translucent indigo glazed through her eyes and sparks pushed through her fingers into the ground, instantly charring the grass in a ten-foot diameter around her. She pulled the electricity with her as she rose to her feet and looked skyward at her attackers.

One by one, the ravens dive-bombed her, each one able to avoid the balls of electric fire she hurled their way. Yalé watched from the water, enthralled by her friend's

abilities. Again and again, the relentless birds took aim, and except for a singed wing, Sam missed them every time. Exhaustion was setting in. She had never used so much of herself, of her powers—not even when she saved Ash and Cinder, not even when she saved Ted.

The ravens sensed her weakening and rallied above, ready to attack all at once and take out the threat. All but one, which Sam saw starting its dive.

Mustering every last bit of energy, Sam reached to the skies and unleashed a lightning storm. Bolts flew in every direction, super-heating the air and incinerating the birds. Most fell into the water and washed away with the current. Some landed on the ground near her. All were dead.

Sam dropped to the ground, depleted.

Behind her, screams began to erupt in the water. "Yalé!" One raven had made it through unscathed and took sight of easier prey. Sam was helpless to do anything.

The bird was strong—beyond that of a real bird—and lifted Yalé, who had transformed back to an Ijiraq in mid-air, hoping the bird would let go. The raven made it only a few feet when it dropped its grip on the girl: the bird's head hitting the ground, its body too . . . several feet away.

Yalé splashed back into the water as a large hand—no, hoof—extended into the river and pulled her to safety. She knew immediately who stood before her with the bloodied antlers, though she had never seen him before as an Ijiraq. "Brother. Deyo!"

The siblings embraced. Sam forced herself to her feet and joined them. "Thank you, Deyo," she said.

"We saw the creatures flying past the village. I knew it was you, but I didn't know it would be you too, sister. I always hoped this day would come." They continued the reunion a few moments longer. "Let's get you back home and get you warm. Are we hungry?"

The girls laughed in their joy and allowed themselves to cherish the moment, though a new level of danger would undoubtedly be coming. They were hungry, and they needed to rest.

They had survived this battle, but Sam would need to regain her strength for the coming war.

CHAPTER SIXTEEN

In and out of sleep for more than 24 hours, Jack sat up
and rubbed his groggy eyes expecting Lee Ezerza to
order him to take it easy and lie back down. He tilted
his head to the side, but it wasn't Lee watching over him any
longer.

Jack looked to the chair Lee had occupied since Deyo
had laid him in bed. "Sam?" He scraped the bugs from his
eyes, grabbed his glasses, and swung his legs over the edge
of the bed. Had he planted his feet, he wouldn't have fallen
backward and hit his head at the sight of his daughter . . .
alive.

"Dad! Are you okay?" Sam said, jumping to his aid.

"Sam, is it really you? How . . . ?" He touched his
daughter's face, caressing her hair and cheeks. He was
having difficulty believing this was real, so he squeezed
tight, afraid to let go.

"I had a friend on the inside. She helped me escape."

"A friend? One of the other kids?"

"A kid, yes. Tahltan, no. Her name is Behgehyale, but I call her Yalé for short. You'll meet her soon. She's Deyo's sister."

"Deyo's sister . . . an Ijiraq helped you?"

Sam nodded. "They're good, not like the others."

"But how did you get back here? How did she free you?"

"Before I explain, there's something I have to show you first," Sam said, and Jack offered a look of skeptical curiosity.

"Okay."

"Are you ready?" He nodded. "Okay, now don't freak out, but it turns out I have other abilities, more than what we knew about."

Sam took a few steps back to give herself room and Jack watched, slightly horrified, as Sam began to twist, and contort, and change. When she was finished, Jack was speechless, looking at a mirror image of himself. He attempted to say something, anything, but the words were stuck in his throat. The astonishment caused his doppelganger to erupt in laughter, but he wasn't finding the humor in what his eyes showed him.

Sam decided to have a little fun at his expense. "Now go to your room, Princess, and don't come out until you've learned your lesson or no supper for you." She was in hysterics at her own imitation, though Jack had never said anything like that to her.

190

"Sam," Jack finally choked out, "How? Where did this come from?" He still wasn't laughing.

Seeing that he was a bit freaked out, Sam transformed back. "Yalé taught me. I can shape-shift, just like one of them. I guess I'm part Ijiraq now," she panned, lifting her hands above her head to imitate horns, laughing.

Jack chuckled, "This is incredible, Princess, but I'm still confused."

"Well, I can't be completely sure, but it seems I can mimic the powers of other magical creatures." Sam explained the apparent link with Ash—her pyrotechnic and telepathic abilities; and now possessing the magic to shape-shift into any living thing.

"Anything?"

Sam knew what he was asking, and though hesitant, she obliged. "Anything," said Sam. She shifted and Jack was face to face with Nan physically standing before him, just as she once was, and every bit as beautiful.

"Can I . . . ?" Jack asked, reaching out his arms.

Sam approached her dad and pulled him in. The awkwardness was apparent, but she knew her dad needed this, especially after all he'd been through: from losing his wife and daughter; to having all three of them in the same room . . . sort of.

Jack steadied his nerves and accepted the hug from his wife—daughter. Nan felt the same. She smelled the same. He didn't want to let go, and in his exuberance, was

squeezing a bit too much.

"Dad . . . Dad, you need to ease up."

"Oh, I'm sorry, sweetie." He released his grip and stepped back, still in awe at who stood before him. A short chuckle as he wiped his eyes dry, "Can you try not to call me Dad while you look like, well . . . ? It's a bit strange if you know what I mean."

"It's all a lot strange," said Sam, who quickly shifted back into her own body. "Now, don't abuse my powers, but I'd be happy to show Mom every now and then."

"Deal."

Sam would recount she and Yalé's harrowing escape in exacting detail. Jack didn't ask a single follow-up question—father and daughter were reunited. That was all that mattered.

As the evening wore on, the townspeople were instructed to stay indoors. The council expected swift and excessive retaliation.

"We can't just sit around waiting for the inevitable," said the youngest councilmember. "If we don't take the fight to them, they'll wipe out our whole village. Telegraph Creek cannot become the epicenter for this war."

Deyo said, "He's right, but it won't matter where it starts; the Ijiraq will destroy this village and everyone in it,

regardless. They are merciless."

The council talked amongst themselves, brainstorming, searching for a plan that didn't end with their extinction. Rose was adamant about surrendering herself, about being the sacrifice that would calm tensions and return some semblance of normalcy to the tribe. Had Sam been in the room, the objections would have echoed through the valley. Rose knew it was the only way, and she used the reunion with Jack as an excuse for Sam's absence.

Grumblings crossed the room. Deyo spoke, "If this is what Dene wants for her people, then we should all respect her decision and her leadership."

The grumblings receded, as no one offered a competing plan—one that didn't end in a massacre. "Then it is settled," said Rose. "We will leave at once. Deyo will escort me to their camp."

The council said their goodbyes to their longtime leader.

"I expect you will celebrate my life and throw a big shindig in my honor," she said with her usual chuckle. "I will be watching over all of you." With that, the door slammed shut, and Rose and Deyo proceeded toward the Ijiraq camp.

"Will you not say goodbye to Sam, Dene?" asked Deyo.

"I don't feel that's wise. She's still young and impulsive and has a long way to go to master her powers. If she knew what we were about to do, she'd be rash. Take care of her, Deyo. Help her learn how to lead, how to be strong and wise in the face of adversity, to think before she acts."

"She's definitely got the strong part down." Deyo laughed a deep belly laugh, and Rose joined in. The remainder of the trip through the forest was quiet, as Rose reflected on her life and everything she'd accomplished for herself and her people. She was at peace.

As much as Sam enjoyed the mini reunion with Jack, she intended to be part of the planning and made her way toward the council chambers. Night was falling on the village and the hallway leading to the backside of the tribal hall with its flickering light made her uneasy. The grimy windowpanes lining the hall and the waning light outside made the corridor feel haunted. Sam was waiting for the Doll-in-the-Hall to make an appearance—a bit of fun her dad used to have during October, hiding a creepy doll in various spots around the house and scaring the bejesus out of her.

Sam made it down the shorter, first section of the hallway and turned left down the long narrow corridor to the grand ballroom. The alcove at the adjacent corner of the intersecting paths was pitch-black. It extended only ten feet to a door that emptied behind the building. She looked

toward the door but saw nothing—*no doll*. She searched her mind for the thoughts of someone or something lying in wait.

Nothing.

Sam walked full speed, wanting to expel the discomfort and anxiety as quickly as possible—she'd feel safe in the expanse of the ballroom, on the other side of the corridor. She continued to search behind her for an approaching predator, a soft glow emanating from her hands, ready to defend herself if necessary.

She reached the door and pushed hard, ready to burst through to safety, but the doors were locked and the force caused her to recoil several steps. Sam's momentum stopped abruptly as she bumped into a stocky being standing in the darkness behind her. She whipped around, her hands and eyes an icy blue, ready to ward off her attacker. She recognized the man; she had seen him around town with his daughter, but they had never spoken.

"What?" was all that Sam could get out when the double doors to the ballroom burst open. She swung back, ready to escape the creepy tall man, but Maddie stood in her way—her eyes washed in hunter green, her own fireball cocked and ready for its target. Sam couldn't tell if it was for her or the man.

The man grabbed her from behind, holding her wrists in an attempt to control her powers. It worked briefly, until Sam closed her eyes and shifted into Puck, causing the brute to drop her, but he quickly grabbed the otter and held it tight.

Maddie knocked Sam out with the fireball. She held back on purpose; the longing to end her wouldn't have had the desired effect.

Sam woke moments later; she was still Puck and enclosed in a chicken wire cage, with barely even enough room to turn her head. She struggled to move, and it forced out a squeak. Tall Man carried her with Maddie by his side, somewhere deep in the forest.

"Oh, I see someone is awake," quipped Maddie. "I'm not sure where you learned to do that Ijiraq trick, but try it again and you'll regret it." Maddie produced a threatening fireball to make her point, and the man shook the cage violently for additional effect.

Sam stayed quiet and calm. Why was Maddie doing this? Maddie must have blocked her ability to sense the man in the shadows. What was his connection, and why would he be helping her? Where were they taking her?

They walked for some time in total darkness, but when Sam spied the rock which contained the heart and locket, she knew exactly where they were and where they were going. She attempted to communicate with Maddie telepathically, but she was shut out. The best she could do was squeak in anger, though it was accompanied by more cage-rattling every time she did.

The travelers reached the ridgetop overlooking the

encampment and were met with the sights and sounds of a ceremony—*the* ceremony.

Nana Rose was tied to the maypole in a similar white gown as Sam had donned. Chanting—a haunting yet beautiful chorus—filled the ravine below. Sam was helpless; she could only watch. She spied Deyo standing behind his father. *Traitor!* she transmitted, but he didn't remove his solemn, downturned gaze.

Sam began to squeak and squeal as loud as she could, but the singing and incantations by Dene Kazune drowned her out. She watched in horror as a wispy, white column of smoke—a ghost—was extruded from Rose's nose and mouth and encircled the tribe before settling inside the ceremonial urn held by the Dene. Her grandmother's head fell to the side. She was gone.

Maddie hadn't said a word throughout. With Rose—and soon Sam—gone, she would reign over the Tahltan. Sam continued squeaking and scratching at the cage. The timbre of the ceremony had ended, and all heads turned toward the ridge.

Deyo ran toward them at full speed, noticing his previous form trapped in the cage being held up high for offer by the man. Deyo recognized him, the same man who refused to join their fight to save the children—his own daughter—because it meant following one of them into battle.

"Stop!" Dene Kazune commanded Deyo, who fell to

his knees halfway up the hill. "What is the meaning of this intrusion?"

"I have something you want. I'm here to bargain on behalf of my people," said Maddie.

"You're too late, young one. Our deal is complete. Rose offered her life for the safety of your people. There will be no further attacks. The eighty-year pact has been restored."

"Not good enough," she said. "I want peace for my people forever, and I have a life that will provide the Ijiraq with all the power they need to return to Karavan and reclaim your rightful place in your homeland."

The man held up the cage again, rattling around the diminutive animal.

"What makes you think we want to return to a place where we were persecuted without mercy? We were hunted and killed for our horns because of the power they possessed, which others used for their own purpose." Dene shook his head. "Leave us, little girl. This is our home now."

Maddie was frustrated, her eyes beginning to glow. Her hands heated up.

Dene Kazune continued, "I suggest you do as I say and not do anything to upset the balance. We have what we need." He held up the vessel containing Rose's spirit.

Maddie capitulated, "Fine, you can have her anyway." She nodded to the man, who threw Sam and the cage tumbling to the bottom of the hill. "But we share the Stikine

Valley, peacefully . . . forever. My people should not have to live in fear any longer."

Nagha retrieved the cage just feet ahead of Deyo, who knew if he could free her, Sam could use her powers to escape.

"Very well, Dene Hodzih," said the Ijiraq Chief. Maddie liked the sound of that. "You have a deal, though I expect I will never have trouble from the Tahltan ever again, or we will wipe out your kind once and for all."

Maddie nodded and retreated out of sight with the man. Her first "deal" as Dene of the Tahltan would cement her name in tribal lore as their savior.

Nagha brought Sam to the Chief. "Should we prep her?"

Deyo thundered over before his father could speak. "This isn't right. You got Rose. Sam is innocent."

"Innocent?! She has slaughtered several of our brethren. Her lack of innocence is exactly why I'm agreeing to this deal," Dene Kazune boomed.

"She was defending herself!"

"Enough of this insolence! You are one of them, and you are no longer welcome here. You are an Ijiraq in form only. Goodbye, Deyo." His father turned his back on him and continued with preparations for the unexpected ritual with Sam.

Deyo knew there was nothing left he could do. He had lost Rose, and he was about to lose Sam. He had lost his birth family, and with Maddie in charge, he would lose his adopted clan as well. He crept up the hill and sat on the edge of the ridge, watching from the perch. He would not allow Sam to die alone.

CHAPTER SEVENTEEN

The time had come.

Sam was left caged as a precaution to keep her from shifting—to do so would have been messy and would likely result in her death, or so she assumed. Death by Ijiraq seemed more palatable and a lot less painful from what she witnessed with Rose.

The cage was placed at the bottom of the pole; Deyo continued looking on from above. Without Sam in her human form, the cleansing ritual had to be forgone. It was a risk the Dene accepted, given the immense and eternal nourishment his people would receive.

Sam spotted Deyo sitting, watching, waiting. *How could you betray Nana?* She transmitted.

"You are mistaken, friend. This was her wish, her desire to free the Tahltan," he responded.

Why didn't you talk her out of it? Why didn't you come up with a better plan? Sam was not angry; she simply wanted answers.

"I'm sorry, Dene Tsesk'iye. Every scenario ended with the extinction of our . . . your people. There was no other way. I'm sorry you could not say goodbye to her. But it was her wish for you not to know. She knew you'd try to stop her. She asked me to watch over you, though I've failed in that duty as well."

Then it's time to do your duty, Deyo. Not to me, but to your people, the Tahltan. You must return to Telegraph Creek and stop Maddie. Do not allow her to fill the void left by Rose . . . or me. You can lead them.

Deyo tilted his head. "Me? You expect the Tahltan to follow an Ijiraq? To follow someone who looks like their enemy? Who was their enemy?"

You are not Ijiraq, you are one of us, and they will follow when you show them the kind of leader you are. Please go now, before it's too late.

"I will not leave you to die alone, Dene. I will stay here until . . . "

Sam cut him off, *There is nothing left that you can do here. You are needed back home. Go now, or I'll allow myself to shift and what you'll witness will be quite gruesome.*

Deyo hesitantly nodded and stood as tears welled in his large ruby eyes. He had so much more he wanted to say to her, so much he owed her, but he remained silent and complied.

Deyo shifted. There was only one way to beat Maddie back to camp, and she already had a couple of hours head

start. Sam watched as a large onyx bird appeared before her, booming as it beat its eight-foot wings and lifted off. The raven was gigantic—bigger than any bird she'd ever seen, larger even than the bald eagles which were so commonplace in the Pacific Northwest.

The red-eyed bird circled high above her before retreating toward the village, one last look at the brave young girl, years wiser than her age. A fourteen-year-old child should not have to die for the sins of others.

As he faded out of sight, Deyo allowed the tailwind to push him higher, ruffling his feathers. It was the first time he'd taken this form in eighty years, since his original banishment. He had forgotten the feeling—to soar, to feel perfectly free—but this was not the time to be enjoying himself. There was work to be done. And mourning, thereafter.

The sun was beginning to crest the horizon and the heat on his feathered head encouraged Deyo to fly faster. He put his massive wings to use, flapping without restraint.

As he approached the village, all seemed quiet. A few townspeople were milling about in their daily routines, but given recent events, most chose to remain in the safety of their homes. There was no sign of Maddie or her tall escort.

Deyo circled high and wide searching for the pair, to head them off before they could return, but there were no signs of them.

The bird's instincts kicked in, that sixth sense animals

have when they sense danger. Deyo swooped and dove to his left, barely ducking a small green fireball as it whizzed past close enough to graze his wing. His attention now on the direction of the blast, Maddie came into view, inexplicably standing in the center of the town square. She continued to rain down—or up—her powers, aiming to kill, though she did not wield the strength to do much more than moderate damage to the powerful Ijiraq above.

Deyo continued his dive down and into the trees where Maddie would be unable to find him without lighting up the entire forest. It was cold and wet, but plenty of dead timbers would combust if she continued the barrage in his direction.

He miscalculated.

The impulsive child—the princess in waiting and supposed leader of her people—fired over and over again in his direction. Smoke and flames began to grow, but she was relentless. The villagers gathered as smoke and embers poured into the town. The tall man, already coughing, pulled Maddie back by her shoulder, sending one last fireball skyward, momentarily snapping her from her rage.

Ted was the first to reach the bell near the dais and clanged and clanged and clanged until a volunteer force gathered to battle the fire. Throngs of people gathered, some with buckets and hoses, others with shovels, who flanked the flames trying to build a proper firebreak.

Deyo remained hidden, despite his acceptance by the

masses. He was desperate to help, but feared his presence might only exacerbate the situation . . . until he saw Jack.

Jack ran at full speed toward the smoke and flames. He didn't seem keen on fighting the blaze, but was looking for Sam. She had disappeared during the night and he was convinced Maddie's fit of rage was aimed at his daughter. He was manic to save his little girl; he had just gotten Sam back.

Deyo took notice and bounded through the trees in his native form, ducking under and through low-hanging branches—the ash and embers would have clouded anyone else's vision. There was no other way he could get to Jack before he harmed himself. Deyo took the path of least resistance, the most dangerous path. He hurdled through the wall of flames and tackled Jack to the ground, stopping his progress. It was enough to save Jack, but it left Deyo smoldering in the open, in full view of a charging Maddie and Tall Man.

Mere paces from the creature, Maddie raised her hands, molding another green orb into shape. She launched it at the maimed, defenseless Ijiraq but it missed its mark, instead hitting Jack square in the chest as he dove to block the attack. He fell to the ground, motionless; not quite dead, but dying. His unconscious body labored for every breath, prolonging the inevitable.

Maddie's eyes glowed dark green, careless of the destruction she'd caused or the injury—soon to be death—of her rival's last living relative. Tall Man attempted to pull the girl away. Even he knew she'd gone too far.

Deyo pulled himself up, no longer concerned with himself, and picked Jack up in his arms, plodding to the medical station. Lee Ezerza was nowhere to be found, and Jack's time was running short. Deyo ripped open Jack's shirt to reveal the charred skin and slight indent left by the fireball. The smell, that wretched smell of burning skin, filled the air. Deyo's heightened animal senses were not an asset at the moment.

Outside, the commotion continued, though Deyo could feel a new disturbance. He hesitated, not wanting to leave Jack's side, but there was nothing more he could do for the man.

As he reached the door, he could see a swarm of people encircling a scuffle taking place near the entrance to the grand hall. He looked back toward the forest, where the flames continued, and though smaller and seemingly contained, yells of instructions and pleas for more help echoed from the trees.

Deyo wanted to help, but when he turned his attention back to the crowd, a familiar set of horns grabbed his attention. The tall man stood on the interior of the makeshift fighting pit, holding back concerned villagers, and instigating the fracas: Maddie versus Yalé.

Instantly, everything became quiet as a decibel-breaking bellow erupted from the rear of the crowd. Deyo

made his presence known without exception, and the crowd parted like the Red Sea as he stomped his way toward the epicenter.

"What is this madness!" he barked, speaking more to Yalé than the other two.

Yalé cowered, more ashamed than fearful of her brother's wrath. Maddie, on the offensive—as it always seemed—was ready to take the fight to Deyo, though Tall Man began to back up, wanting no part of the hulking beast, whose huffs were visible in the chilly morning air.

Maddie glimpsed as her cornerman retreated, giving her pause; she held on to her fireball. "Your sister attacked me! I was only defending myself."

Yalé backed toward Deyo for protection, but also in dishonor, having acted more Ijiraq than Tahltan in her fit of anger.

"Lower your defenses now, Maddie. There is no need for this. Our people need us more than ever now."

"Our people? My people! Leave, or I will make you leave." Maddie's hands glowed, though a bit softer.

Deyo said, "Rose and Sam have accepted us into your clan. We renounce the Ijiraq and everything they stand for."

"I am the leader of the Tahltan now, and you are no longer welcome here."

Deyo spoke not to Maddie, but to the crowd, which had grown twice in size in the moments since his deafening roar. "Most of you do not know me. Perhaps you have seen me as Puck, trapped in that form by the deal made between my father and the Tahltan years ago. Rose freed me and accepted me as a member of this tribe, as did young Samantha. Unfortunately, this child," he said, pointing an accusing hoof at Maddie, "saw to it that Sam would not be able to lead you, as Rose had wished. Sam is being sacrificed as we speak—an unnecessary death thanks to Rose's own selfless act. But Maddie made her own deal with the Ijiraq in exchange for Sam."

Hushed tones snaked through the crowd.

"Lies! All lies!" Maddie screamed. "Are you really going to listen to this monster? He's one of them. He can't be trusted."

"I have no reason to lie. No reason to deceive. The only thing I want is peace for this community and freedom from the oppression of my father and the Ijiraq."

"I already made a deal for peace," Maddie said, copping to her evil deed.

"She admits it. She gave up Sam for peace," Yalé blurted from behind Deyo.

"Sadly, my sister is right, as is Maddie. You do have your peace, even if by ill-gotten means," Deyo continued. "But will that peace last in the hands of a child who is unprepared to lead? A child who handed over one of her own—one of us—to achieve that peace? A true leader fights for their people and acts only selflessly, never selfish. So I ask you now, as hard as it may be for some of you, to follow

me, as Sam had wished, in her absence. Allow me to lead you and show you what real peace is, and how to heal and bring our community back together stronger than before."

Deyo's pleas were met with laughter from Tall Man and Maddie followed suit, along with a few onlookers. "You expect us to follow a monster such as you?"

"Would you prefer I take a different form?" He shape-shifted into an exact replica of the man. "Or would you prefer this?" He now looked like Maddie briefly, before shifting back to his original form. "What I look like should not matter. I am one of you, a proud Tahltan, ready to lead."

The tall man and Maddie could sense the crowd debating the question, and grew nervous as they shuffled from the inner circle, making their way to the bell. Maddie clanged the bell repeatedly until the crowd re-amassed in full. She stood tall on the dais above the villagers, nearly all of whom had now arrived save for those few still battling the blaze.

"What say you?" said Tall Man. "It's time to choose your new leader: that hideous creature, or the princess, the rightful heir to the Tahltan throne, granddaughter of Rose, daughter of our brother Daniel."

Slowly, the people dispersed as they gathered around Deyo or Maddie, showing support for their candidate, a relatively even split that only narrowly favored the girl, though others would need to choose upon their arrival from the forest. Of the councilmembers, only the youngest statesman was present, and even he picked Maddie. Lee Ezerza was still unaccounted for, and despite his age, it was believed he was aiding those fighting the fire.

Ted was the last to make his choice. He hesitated for far too long, though his choice should have seemed easy. His belief in Sam and Rose and the trust they placed in Deyo was swaying him until Maddie cleared her throat at his indecisiveness.

"I'm sorry, Deyo. I have to," Ted said remorsefully. Deyo nodded in understanding.

"We will continue this once the others return from the fire," said Tall Man.

By dusk, the fires were more or less out, though a slight glow of embers could be seen at the edge of the tree line. The crews were making their way back to the village, unaware of the earlier proceedings, though family members quickly met them in the square and filled them in. Everyone was accounted for except Lee Ezerza.

The bell rang to indicate the resumption of their civic duties—if you could call it that. People gathered slowly. Some, who had previously voted, chose to stay at home and not witness the aftermath of the final tally. Tall Man did not wait for the stragglers.

"It's time to finish this. Thank you for your bravery to

those of you battling the fires, but now comes the time that you must decide who should lead us into the next era. Please fall in line where you must."

The remaining votes, as earlier, were nearly even. When all was said and done, the tall man and the remaining councilmembers tallied the headcount. It took three counts to reach a consensus.

The youngest councilperson read the results. "By one vote, the Tahltan have made their voices heard: Maddie is our leader. Her commencement and coronation in two days' time will usher in a new era for our people."

Jack hobbled into the crowd from where he had watched the proceedings from the doorway of the medical building. "Mr. Ezerza. Where is Lee Ezerza?" he questioned with a weak voice. Deyo and Maddie couldn't believe Jack was walking upright, let alone addressing them after the blast he'd absorbed. "Mr. Ezerza gets a vote."

Jack collapsed, unconscious. Deyo and some of his supporters—and even a few of Maddie's band—ran to his aid. Maddie and Tall Man retreated, unwilling to help or answer questions about the elder councilmember.

Jack was returned to the bed from which he had inexplicably risen. A younger girl, an assistant to Mr. Ezerza, worked feverishly to stabilize him. Nasal cannulas provided oxygen, and she attached a heart monitor, plus an IV drip to keep him hydrated. Looks bounced around the room between the girl, Deyo, and the councilmembers—though they seemed more concerned by the old man's whereabouts and his vote.

Deyo said, "Go. Find Mr. Ezerza. Yalé and I will stay watch over Mr. Owsian." The council extricated itself at breakneck speed.

Only the girl stayed behind to play nursemaid. Her training had only brought her this far, and she was worried there was not much more she could do without her mentor's wisdom and experience.

Jack continued to struggle but remained stable for the next few hours while a quiet brother and sister sat watch. They excused the young girl as it neared midnight so she could get some rest. She chose to unfold a cot in the main office of the building, to keep near in case she was needed.

"They're not going to let us stay here, Deyo," said Yalé.

"I know, sister. But something tells me that Mr. Ezerza's disappearance isn't a coincidence. He loved and respected Rose too much to allow such a coup."

"You think Maddie is responsible?"

Deyo nodded. "And the tall man. That girl is out of control. The way she so carelessly bargained away Sam's life and then attacked me . . . and Jack. She will put the tribe in danger, but it seems they have said their peace and are willing to follow her, as foolish as it may be. I can't say I blame them; I'm not sure I would have acted any differently if asked to choose a human to lead the Ijiraq."

"But they would have voted for Sam if she were here.

Can't we go get her? Save her? I can get her out of the cage. I did it once . . . "

"It's too late for heroics, Yalé. They were preparing for the ceremony when she requested I leave. No doubt she is gone, and the Ijiraq now have eternal life thanks to her powers. Next to you, Sam is the bravest person I have ever known."

That name—*Sam*—triggered something. Jack, eyes still closed, sat upright in his bed, ripping the IV from his arm and trashing about—a seizure. Deyo yelled for the nurse, who arrived in seconds. Deyo grabbed Jack by the shoulders and forced him to his back, his legs now kicking too wildly for the girl to control alone. Yalé jumped in to help. As his body continued to convulse, they looked at each other in horror. Then the true horror as Jack's body went limp and the unsettling sound of flat lining rang through the building.

The nurse administered CPR for more than ten minutes before Deyo tired of watching the girl's fruitless efforts. He pulled her back from the dead body. "Let him go; there's nothing more we can do."

"Step back," said a voice from the hallway. "Now!"

Deyo turned, incredulous at what he was witnessing. Sam strutted into the room, clearing the three bystanders into the hall. "Dad," she whispered under her breath. "Stay with me."

Sam, as with Ted, clasped her hands and generated a ball of intense blue energy the size of a basketball. Slowly,

she lowered it onto her dad's bare chest, directly on the spot where he had taken Maddie's blast. Pushing. Pushing. Pushing harder still. Sam drove the ball into his chest cavity, its light so bright that it pulsated from within and filled the room in a haunting azure glow.

Sam backed up and waited, the others looking on through the hallway glass. The glow subsided, then extinguished, leaving the room back in its usual flickering fluorescent state. No one moved. No one said a word. Minutes passed. Sam could hear a question bubbling in Deyo's thoughts, and she held up a hand to silence him.

"Dad?" Sam finally asked, and Jack began to rouse, his head moving side to side, his fingers twitching wildly. "Dad, it's me. It's Sam." His eyes slowly opened, and control returned to his limbs.

"Princess?" he said hoarsely, "Where have you been?"

"Don't talk, Dad." She smiled, and he offered a weak one in return before closing his eyes and falling to sleep.

CHAPTER EIGHTEEN

The vigil over Jack continued until dawn. His breathing remained shallow, but he was alive. Deyo, Yalé, and Sam exchanged hugs and pleasantries, but beyond that no words were spoken of Sam's mysterious and miraculous escape and reappearance. Sam was no worse for wear, at least physically—a few scratches and bruises which the nurse cleaned up.

She spent the night worried about her dad and wracking her brain over how she had gotten here—not only back to Telegraph Creek, but the confluence of events that started as an innocent trip to learn about her mom's side of the family. Nan's death. Her dad's death. Ted's death. Rose, and Daniel. It all had to end, but when?

Sam was lost in dread for hours. An occasional comforting hoof on her shoulder from Yalé let her know she wasn't alone. In those moments of disruption, though, she would read her friend's mind and she could see the horror and destruction caused by Maddie and the tall man: the

fires and fireballs, the vote, the aftermath. She was spared the vision of her dad's assault — thankfully, Yalé had not been there to witness it.

Sam searched Deyo's mind, but he could feel her fishing and shut her out on purpose, to spare her the graphics. However, what she did see were fleeting images of Lee Ezerza — images of Maddie's and Tall Man's faces when questioned by Jack in his moment of strength. It never occurred to her that the man who should have been tending to her dad was not there.

"Where is Mr. Ezerza?" she finally spoke.

Deyo offered only a shrug.

The morning light exploded into the hallway through the building's glass doors as the sun crested the far side of the Stikine Ridge. An oversized silhouette appeared — a shadow — unmistakable in its form: a wolf. A wolf so large, it had no trouble peering through the windowed door more than five feet above the floor. Sunlight reflected off the glass to reveal bright golden eyes and streams of drool dripping from its razor-sharp maw.

Sam wasn't scared; she could feel it was injured. It wasn't just drool, but blood. But from what? Was a villager attacked? Was it the wolf's own blood? It collapsed in place, letting out a puppy-like whimper. She didn't think; she just ran to it.

She struggled with the weight of the enormous beast, its soft and graying fur, patchy from a fight and old age.

Deyo took over, moving her aside and lifting the animal with ease. The medical station had only two rooms capable of housing patients, both now occupied, though proper veterinary equipment and experience treating animals were lacking.

It wouldn't be needed.

"Ch'iyone?" said Deyo—a statement more than a question. Sam stared, waiting for more. "This is not just a wolf, but a man. A shape-shifter like us, but not Ijiraq."

"How can you tell? Who is he?" Sam asked.

Deyo lifted open one of the animal's eyes. Blood had replaced the yellow, so solid and deep that even the blackness of the pupil was barely perceptible.

"Just like the Ijiraq," said Sam.

"But not," replied Deyo. "Ch'iyone has become a legend. Not seen since the Great Peace between my father and your great grandfather. This wolf is the one who protects the tribe, the only creature which can strike fear into the Ijiraq. It's believed he disappeared when the peace took away his need to protect the Tahltan."

"So this is a tribe member?" Sam asked, and Deyo nodded. "Okay, but who?"

Deyo looked toward the nurse, a hint of the wolf's identity.

"Mr. Ezerza?" asked the young woman who'd worked side by side with the elder statesman for the past four years, learning everything she could—though never

learning of her mentor's alter ego.

"Aye," Deyo responded.

Sam pushed Deyo aside and went to work, laying healing hands on her grandmother's dear friend. As she did, the wolf became an apparition, and in its place laid Lee Ezerza. Sam continued the procedure until every cut, every scratch, every bruise and blister had disappeared.

The nurse placed a fur blanket over the man—fitting his identity, though it was made of fox—and placed a pillow under his weary head. He opened his eyes and attempted to speak but was too weak from whatever battle he had clearly been through.

"Stay still, sir. You're in the hospital," the young woman said, seeing the confusion in his face.

"Rest. We have much to discuss when you regain your strength, Ch'iyone," said Deyo.

Lee Ezerza's eyes opened wide at the name, a name he hadn't heard in decades. Behind the closed doors of the council chambers, Rose and Lee had discussed Ch'iyone on rare occasions while talking story about their youth, but never had the name been muttered. It brought joyful yet somber memories of glorious days when the threat of a cruel oppressor wasn't hanging over the tribe.

"Maddie," Mr. Ezerza muttered. Sam could read his thoughts, how Maddie and Tall Man had kidnapped him and tied him up. Then she saw the wolf standing on all fours, a broken rope at his feet, moving across the Great Hall.

"She's become reckless. Dangerous," said Deyo, and the old man nodded and coughed an awful cough that shook his whole body.

Sam said, "We will find her and make sure she doesn't do any more damage."

"Stay," said Lee Ezerza.

"Yalé and I will go and find the girl. Keep watch over him. He may be our only hope against the Ijiraq," Deyo warned.

Sam took minor offense to the comment, believing in her powers more than Deyo it seemed, but simply said, "Go," and turned her attention back to the old shaman. "What happened? You know how I got here, don't you?" Sam was a bit self-absorbed, but the man obliged her youthful narcissism.

"Shh. Watch and listen," he said, closing his eyes.

Sam began to concentrate on his thoughts—on Ch'iyone's thoughts. She could see his visions as he saw them, through the sharp-eyed gaze of the wolf. It hit her that she was no longer just a reader of thoughts but could see memories as if watching them on television. She had performed the trick earlier when she saw the events of yesterday through her shape-shifting friend's eyes, but it hadn't dawned on her; it seemed so natural. Another power granted by the mythical creatures she'd spent an inordinate amount of time with. An Ijiraq ability—the same used against her to project the image of her mother standing before her. A form they couldn't have shifted into unless they had seen into her memories.

Lee Ezerza coughed and another struggling fight for air snapped Sam back to the task at hand.

She was the wolf, and she watched as if reliving her own memory. Creeping to the top of the ridge overlooking the encampment and lying down, she could feel the frozen ground on her belly — on Ch'iyone's belly — facing the view of the ceremony. She was watching herself, the otter, stuck in the cage, barely able to move, her eyes wide . . . scared and shaking.

Her own memories flooded in, the last thing she remembered before passing out from fright. The next thing remembered was running through the trees as fast as a . . . caribou. She could feel the weight of the horns on and the thundering of the ground beneath her hooves. She had shifted to escape, *but why an Ijiraq?* Surely there were far swifter forms she could have taken.

Sam continued watching her life through the wolf's eyes. The chants from Dene Kazune resonated through the valley as Nagha unchained the cage from the maypole and walked the unconscious otter above his head, along the inner circle of the hungry beasts waiting for a taste of the mighty magician's life force.

She wondered why the wolf did nothing to stop the ceremony. If he was as powerful as Deyo said and these monsters were so fearful of him, why didn't he step in to

save her?

Nagha returned to the pole at the center of the camp, the same pole where Rose had taken her last breath, and Sam could feel the heaviness in Ch'iyone's chest as he began to breathe more deeply. A growl, low and heavy, reverberated through the wolf's body, but he remained motionless, only watching.

Dene Kazune's chants grew to a crescendo. Sam didn't know why, but these chants and incantations differed from those used on her grandmother. It didn't matter; like her grandmother, Sam's life force began to pour from her nose and mouth, and even her eyes. The swirls of blue-green energy swept through and over the Ijiraq, causing them to jolt upright, throwing their heads back toward the sky.

They consumed her. She filled them up. Sam wasn't just sustaining them; she was making them more powerful with each breath of her essence. It should have stopped by now, but Sam's energy flowed like a burst pipe. It was too much for them and Dene Kazune realized, almost too late, that his people were getting dangerously drunk—toxic levels of the life energy he never realized were possible.

"Retreat!" the chief yelled, though most continued to imbibe. They couldn't stop. They didn't want to.

Nagha attempted to help, making rounds throughout the tribe, snapping his brethren to reality and forcing them to their tents. Sam's powers continued to drain at an unceasing pace, and those who did not heed the Dene's call began to drop dead. Nearly two-thirds of the Ijiraq tribe was wiped out.

Then Sam felt it, the wolf rearing back on his haunches and the pounce, as she watched Ch'iyone bound down the hill, sights set squarely on the cage. Sam's energy surrounded the wolf but did not affect him in the same way. No, she could feel herself—feel the wolf—getting stronger, breathing easier, running faster . . . energized by her essence.

When Ch'iyone reached Sam, he ripped open the cage and freed her from the prison, carefully grabbing her by the scruff and carrying her toward the forest on the far side of the village. They had almost made it to the tree line when the wolf tripped, launching Sam from his mouth into the brush. He turned his head to see what sent them flying. Nagha came into full view.

A clash of titans erupted as the two beasts snarled and swiped at each other, circling until one of them made the first strike. Nagha went on the attack, landing several blows with his hooves, his entire weight coming to bear on the wolf's head. Ch'iyone stumbled back, trying to regain his vision, blurred from the repeated attacks. Nagha couldn't have known who this particular wolf was, or he would have turned tail.

Ch'iyone gathered himself, shook off the dirt and leaves as a wet dog does, and launched himself at the monster, ripping into his flesh, chunk after chunk. Nagha bleated in agony, a defensive swipe of his horns giving him

the space to fall back and calculate his next move and recover, if only for a minute.

The wolf forced the wounded Ijiraq's decision: Lee Ezerza briefly returned to his human form, then back to the animal.

"Ch'iyone!" Nagha screamed, ensuring he was heard throughout the camp. He ran fast, retreating to the safety of their numbers, decimated as they were.

The wolf returned to Sam's side; she started to rouse. He shifted once again, not wanting to frighten the girl. "Sam," he said. "Wake up, dear. We need to get you out of here." Sam had not remembered this. "I need you to turn into one of them and run as fast as you can back to Telegraph Creek. Do you understand?" Sam nodded. "Then go, and do not stop."

She could feel the weakness—the lack of magic—in her bones as she transformed into a perfect doppelganger of Yalé. Sam ached but slowly pushed herself to her feet, turned to Lee Ezerza, and nodded. She could see the mortal wounds seeping through his torn clothing but complied with his instructions.

Sam hit full speed in a matter of a few strides. They were quick and long, and before she realized it, she was standing on the edge of the dark, quiet village—back in her own memories.

Sam pulled back from Lee Ezerza's mind. "I . . . I'm not sure what to say." She was thankful to be alive, though so many questions were unanswered.

Mr. Ezerza requested one last audience in his memories. Sam watched as he dragged himself deep into the forest, as far away from the Ijiraq as he could get. It was deathly cold—near freezing—and his tattered clothes were doing nothing to keep him warm. She could feel the blood pulsating from his injuries. He finally found a small outcrop of rocks that provided a wind break, crawled underneath, and transformed into the wolf. He would not freeze, though he was more likely to succumb to the wounds Nagha had inflicted. The memory went black as the wolf closed his eyes and drifted to sleep.

Sam wanted to ask why he didn't move to rescue her sooner. Why didn't he use his powers—the threat and might of Ch'iyone—to vanquish them? Why did he let her (almost) die? She reserved herself and simply said, "Thank you," and hugged the shaman, who quickly fell asleep. Though Sam healed his injuries, the old man was exhausted.

A knock on the hallway glass snapped Sam back to attention. The nurse motioned for her, Deyo and Yalé by her side.

"Dene, Maddie and Tall Man are gone. We checked the entire village. Yalé took to the skies and could see them . . . they are almost at the Ijiraq camp," said Deyo. "I'm not sure of their intentions. They couldn't possibly know you're still alive."

"Mr. Ezerza," said Sam. "They're going after him.

They tied him up in the tribal hall to keep him from interfering. It's why he used the power of Ch'iyone . . . to escape. They must have assumed he was going to try and save me." It was a presumptuous statement, but not wrong.

Deyo continued, "Then I guess it's a good thing you're both here. But it won't be long until they're told what happened."

"Maybe Dad will be so mad he'll take care of our problem for us," snipped Yalé.

"Sister, we are Tahltan now. We do not wish harm to anyone anymore," Deyo scolded, and Yalé hung her head in apology. Sam provided a comforting hand, letting her friend know she felt the same way.

"So, what now?" asked the young woman. She wanted to help and be part of the plan, but it was not her fight.

Sam said, "Stay with Mr. Ezerza and help him recover as fast as possible. We're going to need his help. If my dad is feeling up to it, have him help you when he wakes up." The nurse nodded. "We should probably get the council together and figure out our next move."

"The Ijiraq will not sit idly by; I expect they will attack swiftly," said Deyo.

"Well, at least we have the numbers now," Sam retorted coldly, causing Deyo to pry for an explanation. Rather than explain, Sam showed her friends the memories she now possessed. The images horrified and relieved them—a strange sensation that wasn't sitting well.

"Enough," Deyo said, interrupting the visions of old friends-turned-enemies perishing. "Let's get to the chambers." Deyo was disgusted by what he'd witnessed, but knew it would give them the advantage they needed to survive.

As the glass doors shut behind them, a steady tone filled the hallway and the sounds of a machine whirring to life were followed by a thump. The flat tone continued. Another thump, and the lights flickered.

"What's going on?" Jack was awakened by the commotion, the constant ringing.

He made his way across the hall and to the nurse standing there over Lee Ezerza. Defibrillating paddles in hand, she let the flatline of the machine provide her answer.

CHAPTER NINETEEN

The council formed their plan. The Ijiraq, despite their thinned numbers, were still capable of decimating the Tahltan, but the Tahltan still had the advantage: they had Sam, and they had Ch'iyone . . . until they didn't. Jack burst through the council chamber doors and blew up their plans with the news of Mr. Ezerza's passing.

Sam jumped up, ready to revive him or at least try. "We can't do this without him," she said through tears.

"I'm sorry, Princess," lamented Jack.

"We have to move on without him, Dene," said Deyo. "Even if you healed him, he'd be too weak. And now Nagha knows he's vulnerable and can be hurt."

"I have to try," she said. Sam slammed through the double doors and ran to the medical station.

A sheet had already been draped over the man's head. The nurse was nowhere in sight. Sam swiped the sheet from his body and it floated ghostily to the floor. Still weak from reviving her dad and healing Ch'iyone's wounds, Sam

pushed through, creating a ball of energy which she submerged into Mr. Ezerza's chest. Again and again she tried, until finally a shallow inhale rose in Lee Ezerza's chest. His eyes remained closed, and the subsequent exhale held one simple command: "No. You be Ch'iyone." He didn't draw another breath.

"What do you mean? I'm Ch'iyone?" Sam, confused, drove all of her remaining strength through the old man's body. She passed out from the effort, but the man remained dead.

Sam awoke to the aroma of mushroom soup—she hated mushrooms, but she was starving, and it smelled almost palatable. The bowl of piping hot liquid sat on the desk in her room. Jack and Deyo were there to greet her.

"Eat, Dene. You are weak, and you must regain your strength for what is to come," said Deyo. Jack supported Sam's elbow as she sat upright and slowly made her way to the table.

She turned her nose up at the smell but gulped the bowl to get it over with, nearly scalding her throat. Jack produced a small loaf of sourdough bread which she also devoured, but at least enjoyed despite the dryness.

"Mr. Ezerza?" she asked.

"He's gone, Princess. I'm sorry."

The old man's last words played on repeat through her head. She opened her mouth, ready to tell them what was said, but reconsidered.

"Have you found Maddie and the tall man?"

"Yalé hasn't returned yet, though I expect her back any time."

"And when do we think the Ijiraq will attack?"

"It's hard to say. A day, maybe two. If I know my father, he will be extra cautious now that he has fewer soldiers. But make no mistake, he will be prepared, and when he gives the order, it will not be pretty. He will be unrelenting in his malice."

"I won't risk this village or its people. We should leave. Evacuate to a safe location where the Ijiraq can't find us."

Jack spoke, "Where are we going to hide that many people, though? If we head back to Dease Lake, they'll see us, and we'd be putting even more lives in danger if they follow us."

Deyo said, "I know of a place, but it will take a few days to get there. It's about 30 kilometers to the south. We'll need to hurry to avoid the next storm."

"Show me."

"Like I said, Dene, it's quite a trek."

"Then we better make it fast." Sam shifted into a raven. She began to caw at her dad, who shook his head, not understanding. *Tell the council of our plans and have everyone ready to leave by tonight,* she transmitted for both Jack and

Deyo to hear. *As soon as we get back, we'll go.*

Jack nodded and left. Deyo scooped up the bird, carried her outside, and matched her form. He was double her size, but they beat their wings in unison and became airborne.

I'm flying. This is . . . wow! Sam thought. It was natural as she floated in formation behind Deyo. Sam was overcome by emotion, the weightlessness not only from the air under her wings, but for the briefest moment she was able to let go of all the pain and torment she'd endured in her young life. If she could stay in this form forever, she'd be free. The thought was liberating, though it was soon followed by the image of eating animal carcasses and insects. Her freedom would have to wait until her people were emancipated from the Ijiraq.

As the two birds crested the ridge on the far side of the Stikine, a massive volcano emerged before them. Mount Edziza was one of Canada's most prominent peaks and loomed large over the region, still active and pumping magma throughout its chambers.

A volcano? Sam asked incredulously. Her sharp bird eyes homed in on steam pouring from various exhaust openings on the side of the mountain.

It has not erupted in several hundred years, Dene. There are caves—lava tubes with hot springs large enough to hold the entire tribe and keep them warm. Deyo could sense her continued hesitance as they drew closer. *This area was once*

very important to the Tahltan. It is here that they mined obsidian for weapons and tools, though I doubt anyone from the tribe has been there in a hundred years.

Sam recalled the décor in the tribal hall entrance—several jet-black objects: knives, arrows, and spears attached to notched wood of various lengths and bound with rope, sat in a glass case. They appeared as sharp as the day they were crafted; the light glinting off them ominous. She had no idea they were so old.

As they reached the mountain they swooped over the snow-capped caldera, which reached over nine-thousand feet, then raced lower on a downdraft around several cinder cones, some of which vented steam causing Sam's eyes to briefly fog over. The stench of rotten eggs was palpable.

Deyo led Sam to the volcano's north side, where they landed and returned to their usual forms. The mountain was mostly desolate, with a few scattered boulders and some brush which pushed up through the volcanic rock. The landscape looked more like Mars than Earth.

"This way," Deyo commanded. "Careful of your steps; the dirt can be slick, especially when it's wet."

Sam noted the red and black soil, and her footprints. She twisted the ball of one foot from side to side, testing her hold. *Seems firm.* Sam's next step landed her on her butt, and she wished she had heeded Deyo's warning.

Deyo helped the young lady up as she gave him a sarcastic look of thanks and wiped red clay from her behind.

He laughed in return.

Deyo pointed to a hole a few hundred feet away, near the base of a relatively small but steamy cinder cone. The opening was smaller than Sam had expected, measuring five feet wide by three feet tall. It reminded her of the hovel on the backside of the heart-shaped rock where she'd first discovered Ash in Arizona. He would have loved it here.

Something gnawed at Sam. "How exactly do you know about this place? If it's been abandoned for hundreds of years . . . "

"I never said it was abandoned. But, yes, the Tahltan have not used this site since well before your grandmother was born. When the Ijiraq first came to this world—from Karavan— this is where we first sought refuge."

"So, you expect us to hide in a place that your father knows about? Are you insane?!"

"It's a calculated risk, Dene. There is no ideal situation here. There is nowhere else to hide that doesn't leave our people exposed." Deyo was right and she knew it, but she still didn't like it. "If we leave under cover of darkness, we can avoid their sentries. Yalé and I can patrol overhead until the tribe gets out of the valley. If we see a sentry nearby, we'll ensure it's taken care of."

"Show me," Sam insisted, nodding toward the cave. Deyo shifted into Puck, his antlers and broad stature far too large to squeeze through the opening. Sam followed suit, though her slender frame could have easily fit.

Sam's eyes adjusted almost immediately, and just in time to catch herself as she slid down the wall of the cave entrance. It was slick from steam, but the drop was a mere three feet. From there, the lava tube opened into a cavernous space which descended deeper into the volcano. The tube presented two separate offshoots, and Deyo motioned Sam toward the left one.

"As good as your otter eyesight is, it won't hold up in these dark spaces. Shift," he requested and returned to his Ijiraq form. Sam followed—a perfect replica of Yalé. Her now glowing ruby eyes pulled in every last photon of ambient light. She imagined this was what it would be like to wear night-vision goggles, though instead of the eerie green incandescent glow, she saw various shades of red. "The left is more habitable. The right side is where the hot springs are."

"Well, don't we want to go there then? Wouldn't it be warmer?"

"Aye, Dene. Much warmer . . . and deadlier. Smell the air," he demanded. "That rottenness is sulfur dioxide from the springs. It's toxic. The cave opening is just enough to circulate the air and keep the steam from filling this space."

"Left it is."

The slick descent into the tube was slow; they both lost their footing more than once, catching themselves on the rocks. Deyo explained how the rock path was already there when the Ijiraq arrived. Rose had confirmed to him that the Tahltan placed them there to ease their way in and out of the space. A few toppled *inuksuk* could be seen as well.

The ceiling expanded above them as the cavern widened and flattened out before ascending back up into the mountain even deeper. "Here," said Deyo. "This area will be sufficient to hide the tribe. Any deeper, and we run the risk of the tunnel collapsing into a magma chamber."

Sam inspected the area. It meant cramped quarters for her people, but they would be safe.

"Dene," Deyo called to her. "Look at this."

Sam's giant red eyes grew larger. Cave paintings. Crude, but unmistakable—a girl holding fire, then transforming into a bird, and then again . . . into a wolf.

"There's no way."

"If it were prophesized, then perhaps this is you."

"Prophesized by whom? That could be anybody . . . Rose?" After Lee Ezerza's dying statement that she was Ch'iyone, Sam knew it wasn't her grandmother.

"Ijiraq folklore warns of the coming of the Raven-Wolf Queen. It's from these drawings that the legend was born. That this queen would banish them back to Karavan, where they would once again be subjugated by more powerful creatures."

Resigned to her supposed fate, Sam told Deyo of the old man's proclamation. "This can't be, but Mr. Ezerza told me to be Ch'iyone. I've never transformed into a wolf. Not to mention, Rose said I'm part of the Raven clan." She was

234

grasping for excuses to avoid the truth.

"Perhaps Dene Rose did not know. Have you tried to shift into a wolf? Perhaps you should."

Sam shrugged and began to concentrate. Her Ijiraq form decomposed, but not into anything resembling a wolf. Again and again, nothing. She shifted into her human form, believing that might help. Try as she might, she could not shapeshift into the legendary wolf.

"See, that's not me!"

Deyo nodded. "I suppose not. Perhaps it was just meant to scare the Ijiraq into behaving in this world. It seems they never learned."

"Let's go. We need to get back and make sure everyone is ready to go."

Sam's insistence on who she might or might not be tore at her throughout the journey home. Not a word was spoken or transmitted between them for the entire flight.

As they crossed the river, the hustle and bustle of the townspeople was apparent. The scattering was purposeful and urgent, and not a soul showed any signs of panic. Yalé met her brother and Sam at the dais, where they continued to oversee the preparations.

"There's no sign of Maddie or Tall Man," said Yalé. "Wherever they are hiding, it's out of view from above."

"I don't think we need to concern ourselves with them any longer," replied Deyo, as Jack and the youngest council member joined them. "How close are we?"

The young man looked at his watch and nodded to Jack, who proceeded to ring the bell three times in succession. "They have one hour to gather here with only the essentials."

"Yalé and I will stay behind to patrol for prying eyes above," said Deyo.

"Councilman Owsian and I will see to it that no one is left behind," said the young man. Sam glanced side-eyed at her dad with the slightest smirk, which didn't go unnoticed. "The rest of the council thought it appropriate to make Jack a member. After all, Dene, the father of the queen should have some say in tribal matters."

Queen?

After hearing the story of the Raven-Wolf Queen, she wasn't sure she liked the ring of it anymore. But she was their queen—or would be once the coronation ceremony commenced. Until then, she was just a figurehead, someone the tribe would follow in the absence of true Tahltan leadership. They all believed in her, even if her own doubts said otherwise.

The hour passed in a flash. Deyo and Yalé took to the air, checking one last time for signs of Ijiraq raven-sentries or ground troops before sending the all-clear signal to move out.

The caravan departed Telegraph Creek in two

soldierly, parallel columns; first heading downriver to the west, then across an old footbridge spanning the Stikine, and finally south toward the volcano. They would walk until dawn.

Sam scouted ahead and found a dense thicket of pines capable of hiding the masses from any downward-looking eyes.

It was the prying eyes of two of their own, though, sitting under an outcropping of rocks on the hilltop adjacent to the bridge, which went unnoticed.

Maddie pointed to Mount Edziza in the distance. She had been there a few years earlier with Nana Rose and Lee Ezerza, as part of her training. She knew where they were going, and she knew of the legend of the Raven-Wolf Queen—a legend she was destined to fulfill.

CHAPTER TWENTY

The journey across the Stikine Valley toward Mount Edziza was treacherous, and not one ever made by any current members of the tribe, save for Maddie. Their progress was slow but steady, moving only as fast as the slowest of their people. They would leave no one behind and they would get there together, but it would not be easy—Mother Nature had other plans.

As dawn broke on the second day of travel, the skies darkened and ferocious winds whipped through the canyon where they had taken shelter for the night. Winter was upon them, and snow not typically seen until well into the season descended upon the unprotected travelers. The night had been cold, but with it, the storm brought sub-freezing temperatures.

The Tahltan were used to the cold. They had lived with it for as long as they had inhabited the valley; it was a way of life. This, however, was different. They were without proper shelter, and many in their haste and need to travel

light had failed to bring adequate apparel. They were exposed in the open, no caves or windbreaks in sight, incapable of building a fire in the freezing gale-force winds. Mother Nature had them dead-to-rights, a seeming ally of the Ijiraq, doing their dirty work for them.

Just then, before a single tribe member could complain, before they felt even the slightest chill, a globe of lime-green light appeared above them and dropped down, encompassing the entire camp. Sam sat at the center of the giant bubble, cross-legged, eyes closed, and chin to her chest in concentration.

Sam held the dome of heat for over an hour; unmoving, her focus never wavered. Slowly. Slowly. Slowly, the safety she provided began to withdraw. The bubble of warmth cooled and drew in until finally, her energy spent, Sam passed out, leaving her people unprotected once again.

Jack and Ted ran to her side to prop her up as the winds started to abate some, but the snow continued to swirl, though with far less vigor. Deyo joined them.

"What are we going to do?" asked Ted.

"I can carry her, but we need to get everyone else to a safe place. Yalé is scouting for shelter as we speak," said Deyo.

Jack said, "Until then, I think we should keep pushing forward. We're too exposed here . . . to the elements and the Ijiraq."

"Aye," Deyo agreed. "They are certainly aware of our

desertion by now and will widen their search until they find us."

Jack gathered the council, and within minutes the caravan was moving toward the safety of the volcano. Deyo shifted into the form of a black-as-night stallion standing a staggering 23 hands tall, carrying Sam over his back, with two elders who had been the slowest among them and needing assistance. Their pace picked up slightly despite the snowfall and ever-growing drifts lining their path.

They continued on for over an hour when Yalé returned with the news. "Keep pushing, brother. Three miles ahead, there is a thick grove of trees lined with boulders. It should be dry enough to keep our fires lit."

Deyo briefly dismounted his riders and shifted back so he could relay the news. His booming voice was enough that the entire tribe—dispersed over a quarter mile—could hear him clearly. "Three miles! Three miles to go! Double-time!"

The four-hundred strong—family—pushed themselves to their limits, moving as fast as possible in treacherous conditions. Yalé followed Deyo's lead, transforming into a large chestnut mare carrying the next three slowest members on her back.

It took them two hours. By the time they arrived, the snow had nearly stopped and the protection of the trees provided shelter and a modicum of warmth. Fires were lit under the canopy of the grove and the entire tribe was safe.

The council convened around the central fire, Sam lying on a bed of branches and pine needles at her dad's side. The youngest councilmember spoke, "We can't keep going like this. It does us no good if we do not get there alive . . . every last one of us. We need to stay here, at least until Sam is back to health."

The council nodded, and Jack looked down at his brave girl, weak from heroism. He worried about his daughter—that she would push herself too far, to a place from which she might not recover. He knew he could not protect her, that she would always give all of herself to do the right thing. He was equally proud and terrified.

With smoke pouring from the treetops, Deyo and Yalé took flight again to ensure they were not being tracked. They would soar nearly five thousand feet high throughout the night, the high winds buffeting their feathers, carving long oval paths between Telegraph Creek and the shelter of pines. There were no signs of Ijiraq, not even a single raven sentry.

Winter in Northern British Columbia meant the sun was taking its time, breaking over the land later each day. Deyo and Yalé returned with the all-clear signal, ready to move out. They were a full day behind schedule and still two days from the safety and protection of Mount Edziza. Sam and the elders once again mounted their trusted Ijiraq steeds as the tribe embarked on another day of travel. The snowdrifts built themselves high through the night, and the two horses trudged through, clearing a path for the others.

Sam opened her weary eyes. She was lying on her stomach and staring at the ground, rhythmically bouncing up and down with each step. "Where are we?" She groggily righted herself on the horse's back.

Jack walked alongside Deyo to keep an eye on his princess. "Good, you're awake. How are you feeling?"

"My head hurts a bit." She rubbed the back of her neck. Deyo whinnied to let her know he was there. She repeated herself, "Where are we? How far are we from the volcano?"

"Two more days," Jack responded. "This snow is slowing us down."

Sam positioned herself upright and began to raise her hands above her head, a slight glow forming when a voice rushed into her throbbing head. *Please, put your hands down, Dene. You must rest. You will need all of your strength. Some things can be done the old-fashioned way, you know?* thought Deyo.

"I can blast us right through this," she argued, "and get us there faster." She doubled over with a sharp wince, lightning and thunder filling her senses. Jack reached up to steady her.

Deyo continued, *Dene, your compassion and need to protect your people is commendable, but if you cannot recover, you will be useless against the Ijiraq if and when they attack.* His candor caught her off guard.

"Useless!" she shouted loud enough for the entire tribe to hear.

"Princess," Jack said. "Please calm down and reserve your energy. Here, you need to eat and regain your strength." Sam reached out and tentatively took the nearly frozen loaf of bread from Jack and began gnawing on it long enough for Deyo to finish what he wanted to say.

I'm sorry, Dene Tsesk'iye, I meant no offense. But the time has come for us to make our stand, and without you—without you at full capacity—we will be decimated. I beg you, please eat as much as you can, even if that means others of us walk in hunger. Without you, these people will die.

"No pressure there," Sam panned, and she shoved another piece of stale bread into her mouth and chewed and chewed. She would not say another word for hours, partly out of stubbornness, partly from not wanting to hear any more about how she was their savior. If she was quiet, she hoped the others would stay that way as well. And they did.

Slowly, Sam could feel her strength and magic returning, juggling a jawbreaker-sized ball of energy back and forth mostly out of boredom. Jack and Deyo attempted to talk her out of using any ounce of magic, but they deigned to her whims after they fell on deaf ears, Sam never offering a semblance of a response beyond a dirty look. At least she was no longer argumentative.

Another chilly night rolled in, and though snowless, sporadic winds whipped and the fires had to be manned constantly to remain lit. The council offered their services so the caravan could rest as much as possible, and took turns tending to the fires. Two-hour shifts allowed everyone to chip in but also get the rest they needed. One more day and they would reach their destination—the top half of a cloud-covered Mount Edziza loomed in the not-too-far distance, bringing hope to the entire camp.

Intense sun greeted the Tahltan in the morning, the air so crisp that ice crystals sparkled and danced in the light. Half-day's travel would bring them to the edge of the forest, to the base of the red, barren slopes of the ancient volcano. It would take the remainder of the day, though, to traverse the sliding sands of the mountain leading to the mouth of the lava tubes.

Sam was restless, still being made to ride on Deyo's maned back, a touch of punishment for an untrusted teenage girl. She pouted the entire time.

"Are we there yet?" Sam whined for the fiftieth time.

"Ah, there it is," cajoled Jack. "Now it's a road trip." Deyo let out a whinny that stampeded through the forest.

Sam rolled her eyes, and Jack handed her yet another loaf to munch on. When this was all over, she would refuse to eat bread for a year, she thought. Not even a good old PB&J. Nope, just eat the peanut butter and jelly straight from the jar.

I think you'll be at full strength by the time we get there, said Deyo. *Keep eating.*

244

"I'm sick of these giant croutons. And I'm stuffed. You're fattening me up like a Thanksgiving turkey," she said. Only Jack laughed.

I don't think a turkey would make a very good adversary against my father, Dene. Sam couldn't help it and let out a guffaw, realizing Deyo didn't understand the American reference. *Did I say something funny?* he asked.

"You wouldn't get it," she chuckled and in a way it reminded her of Nana Rose. "Keep walking, my friend, and I will keep forcing down these apparently strength-inducing carbs. I could use a little spinach right now."

"I never pictured you as much of a Popeye," Jack said, the joke once again falling flat as only he and Sam laughed. She was feeling back to herself again.

The afternoon sun was waning fast in the western sky as the caravan reached the southwest edge of the volcano. It loomed over them, casting a seemingly inescapable shadow. They still had hours of travel to skirt the mountain before making their way up its slopes. Dropping temperatures and the threat of another storm provided a sense of urgency, though Sam decided to hold their position with the council's concurrence.

"We need to stay here for the night," she reasoned. "We can't leave ourselves exposed again."

Deyo said, "Agreed, Dene. With your powers returned, we cannot afford to waste them. Better to stay where we are somewhat sheltered."

"What if we kept going, just a bit farther," said the youngest councilmember. "We can stay undercover of the trees moving south and cut down the time we'll need to travel tomorrow. It'll be slow, but we can stop if needed and make camp."

Sam nodded, though they maintained their position. "Wouldn't north be faster?" she asked, and the young man shrugged. "Deyo, Yalé, and I will check it out first and see." Sam immediately shifted into a raven with Yalé, though Deyo remained an Ijiraq.

"Stay with your people, Dene. Yalé and I will go. You should continue to rest."

"I agree, Princess," said Jack.

Nonsense, Sam transmitted to the entire council. *This is my decision, and I want to see it for myself. Let's go.* Sam was aloft before another person could decry her decision—Deyo and Yalé lagged behind.

The trio swept over the peak riding a frozen current and began to circle. The councilman's desire to take the tribe around the south side was looking more and more like the right move. It was longer but far less treacherous, and her people had been through enough. Safety was paramount. Sam would see to it that they all survived.

South then, Dene? said Deyo.

South, Sam responded. *Yalé, head back and let the others know to move out immediately. Deyo and I are going to do a little advance scouting.*

246

Deyo waited for Yalé to depart before his inquisition. *Dene . . . what are you looking for exactly? What are we scouting for? We know the route well now.*

It's been too quiet, Deyo. Don't you think? Deyo let out a screech in agreement. *I want to search the area and make sure we haven't been followed.*

Lead the way, Deyo said, allowing the young leader to show her burgeoning prowess. He would let her lead and mentor only if needed. If this were a mistake, he would protect her, but not without the lesson unlearned.

Sam made sweeping circles starting at the volcano's peak and spiraled down the mountain, staying wide enough to observe the entire terrain and forest's edge. The coldness of the wind and gently falling snow chilled her despite her coat of feathers, but it didn't avert her concentration.

Deyo followed off her right wing in silence, watchful for any signs of his father's forces.

Did you see that? asked Deyo, who peeled off and pulled up to a higher vantage point.

What is it? I don't see anything.

There was movement in the trees . . . on the edge of the forest near that crater.

Northwest, at the base of Mt Edziza, sat a depression, a pockmark on the side of the massive mountain—a smallish volcanic peak that had collapsed into itself millions of years earlier.

Go in for a closer view? It wasn't so much a question as

it was a command, but Sam hoped Deyo would give her the approval she was seeking.

He said nothing, holding steady until she made her move. He faithfully followed, unsure what danger awaited them and ready to put his life on the line for his chief.

The pair circled, then hovered on an updraft directly above the crater. *I don't see anything, Deyo. I think we should land and check it out on foot.*

Yes, Dene, but we need to be cautious.

Once under cover of the tree line, Deyo returned to his Ijiraq form and Sam to her human form.

"I'm not getting a good feeling about this," said Deyo. "Something is off. I think you should shift into Yalé. It may be nothing, but you'll be faster if we need to escape."

Sam complied, and they began to search the forest. A twitch in the bushes caught their attention, then the crunching of dead leaves and snow moving away from them, but not fast—plodding, careful steps. Not Ijiraq. Not animal. Human.

It took seconds for Sam and Deyo to catch up.

"Maddie?" questioned Sam as Yalé. "What are you doing here?" she said, transforming back into herself.

The fugitives were caught off guard.

Maddie answered, "We were looking for the tribe. We got lost."

"Looking for the tribe? So you can take another of us to be sacrificed?" Sam was incredulous at the girl's brazenness.

"No, that's not true," Maddie demurred. "We want to come back. We . . . screwed up."

"Understatement of the year, wouldn't you say, Deyo?" the sarcasm hiding Sam's fear. "You've decided to be part of the tribe again? So, let me guess, the Ijiraq double-crossed you, and now you want forgiveness and protection?"

Maddie and the tall man nodded. "We're truly sorry," said Tall Man. "We never realized things would go this far. We never intended for anyone to get hurt. We just thought we were doing right by the tribe. We were wrong. Please, accept our apology. We will help however we can to make sure our people remain safe from those monsters." Looking to the hulking creature standing before him, "My apologies, Deyo. You are not a monster. Not one of them."

Deyo gave a half-accepting nod at the apology.

"I'm sorry, Sam. Nana Rose was right; you are the one who should lead us. I just hope you can forgive me. Whatever I can do to prove it to you, I swear I will . . . "

Sam cut her off. "I suppose we'll see, won't we." Sam and Deyo were doubtful of their sincerity, but they didn't have a choice. Maddie and Tall Man were Tahltan, and Sam had sworn to protect all of them—even the two traitors.

Deyo and Sam shifted into horses and allowed Maddie and Tall Man to climb aboard for the relatively short ride to meet up with the rest of the tribe. They had not been too far off course, just five miles north of the main band, though by now they were undoubtedly farther south and complying with Sam's instructions.

Maddie and the tall man continued to apologize and their remorse appeared genuine, but Sam requested silence for the remainder of the ride.

CHAPTER TWENTY-ONE

Maddie and Tall Man watched and waited as the tribe made their way out of Telegraph Creek toward Mount Edziza. Their companion, an Ijiraq messenger in the form of a pigeon, cooed next to them.

Maddie said, "Tell your Dene that they're headed to the volcano, to the lava tubes on the north side of the mountain." The bird began to flap. "But Sam is mine! You tell him that. He can do what he wants with the rest, but not until I'm finished. Understand?" With a final acknowledging coo, the bird departed with Maddie's message.

"What are you going to do with her?" asked Tall Man.

"I'm going to show her that she's not as powerful as she thinks. And if she refuses to leave after that, then I will feed her to the Ijiraq . . . again."

"But you've seen what she's capable of, Dene Hodzih. Why not let the Ijiraq deal with her? The tribe needs you alive."

"So, you think she'll kill me? Is that what you're

saying?" Maddie's retort was all too childlike, with a humph.

"No, not at all. I only want to be sure we have our leader when this is all said and done."

"A leader leads by example. I will show everyone what that looks like when I get rid of the vermin infesting our people."

The tall man didn't bother with a comeback, but knew he would have to watch over and protect the girl at all costs. Her head was swollen and affecting her ability to think logically. He feared her emotions would get her killed.

The Tahltan picked up their travel around the south side of Mount Edziza before dawn—it would be their only way to make it to the shelter of the inner mountain before the darkness of late afternoon.

Maddie and Tall Man's arrival at camp the previous night sent murmurs throughout. A short meeting with the council assured their place, though strong suspicions from Sam and Jack persisted. Maddie's sincerity, however, won over the others. Her openness with her history and knowledge of the lava tubes made her case—she could help, and they needed all they could get. It only made Sam more suspicious. Why had Nana Rose never brought her here? Why had she never even mentioned this place?

Tall Man walked at the back of the pack with Deyo,

where he could see over everyone and keep an eye on Maddie. Deyo noticed his walking companion's overprotective vibe. "She'll be okay . . . you'll both be okay. It's good to have you back," said the taller of the two.

The tall man only nodded, still not comfortable that an Ijiraq walked amongst them and less comfortable, still, that the entire tribe accepted Deyo as one of their own. The lack of trust went both ways, but Deyo would be accepting, despite the man's treasonous behavior. It's what Rose would have expected from him.

The sun had barely risen before dusk was upon them. The weather was crisp, with ferocious winds racing down the barren slopes of the mountain and sandblasting them against the tree line. The tribe moved back into the forest a few hundred yards, providing a small respite from the brunt of gales.

Jack and the other councilmembers leading the tribe threw up their fists at Sam's command to halt the caravan. They had arrived. Deyo and Tall Man made their way to the front, to join them before the short, steep ascent.

Sam shouted as the tribe encircled the council to hear her announcement, "It doesn't look far, but it's slippery. Yalé and I will lead the way. Do your best to follow the footprints of the person in front of you, to avoid falling. If you need assistance, please pair up with someone who can help you make the climb. Most importantly, take your time."

Jack looked on, proud of his daughter's acumen in

such a precarious situation. She *was* Dene Tsesk'iye—the Raven Chief. She had become their leader, a role she was meant for.

Two by two, the tribe lined up and began to make their way up the side of the mountain. Yalé's large hooves dug into the silty earth and created mostly flat indentions, which those who followed could safely step into. It took more than an hour before the last of the Tahltan stepped from the forest: Deyo and Tall Man once again guarding their blindside—the human leaning on a large, sharp-ended walking stick—spear—to steady the climb.

Deyo wanted to lead with his sister, insisting his wider and much larger footsteps would provide more stable footing for the Tahltan. Sam still expected a surprise and wanted him at the back where he could protect anyone who might fall behind. It wasn't the time to question her. He fell in line like a good soldier.

Thirty minutes after Deyo and Tall Man stepped foot from the forest, Yalé and Sam were reaching the lava tube opening. Maddie demanded—politely—that she be first to enter, given her familiarity. She could light the way for the others and help them safely through the small portal and down the short slide to solid footing. Ted asked permission—and was granted such—to follow his sister. Ted

set up lanterns around the perimeter inside the pitch-black cavern, giving them ample light to safely get everyone inside.

Progress slowed as room was shrinking with only half of the tribe inside. Maddie called out to Sam, "I can take them from here. I'll show them the way down the tube and make room for the others."

Sam didn't like the feeling of taking commands from the girl, but she had no choice. She had to get her people inside, and fast. Night had fully set in, and despite the clear skies and full moon, the temperatures were plummeting, and the winds picked up even harder. "Go!" she barked.

Jack and the council got on their posteriors and slid through the slim opening, Jack saying first, "I'm proud of you, Princess. I love you."

"I love you too, Dad. Thank you for bringing me up here. I'll see you inside," she responded. He offered only a toothy grin before sliding out of sight. His excitement reverberated back out of the opening when he laid witness to the beauty of the cave, causing Sam to smile as she locked eyes with Yalé. They chuckled at his childlike giddiness.

Deyo and Tall Man finally made it to the top and aided the last few tribespeople through the portal where Ted and Maddie waited to ensure they got in safely.

"You did it, Dene," smirked a proud Deyo.

"*We* did it. Thank you, friends." Sam offered Tall Man her appreciation, too. "Shall we?"

Yalé transformed into a butterfly and flit through the opening, though the winds made it more difficult than it should have been. As she disappeared, the mountain rumbled and shifted.

"What was that?" Sam asked. "Please tell me this thing isn't about to erupt."

Neither Deyo nor Tall Man had time to answer as a cloud of black sulfuric dust erupted from the cave opening and a series of green fireballs shot out, like fireworks from a cannon.

Sam ignored the danger and slid through the portal opening, Deyo's screams of agony echoing in the chamber as she landed on her feet.

Sam immediately shifted into an Ijiraq, her heightened vision clambering through the dark and dust-filled cave for answers. Deyo's pained bleats continued outside, but Sam's focus was on the masses. She had to block out his cries for help. The right side of the cave had collapsed, perhaps a blessing in disguise given the extreme toxicity emanating from it. She searched for someone . . . anyone.

A set of piercing yellow eyes rounded into form, then the pearly glint of razor-sharp canines . . . *a wolf!* Sam brought her hands—hooves—together, but her fire and energy magic was useless in her form. She sprinted left, deep into the lava tube without care, escaping the menacing jaws bearing down on her.

A wolf? How? Her contemplation was cut short, met by

another set of eyes: ruby—*Yalé!*

A second pair of eyes, identical, though slightly narrow, appeared from behind the first. Sam stopped in her tracks, turning to meet the baritone growl of the wild dog behind her, set to pounce.

"Welcome, dear Sam. Or should I call you Dene Tsesk'iye?" said a voice coming from the narrower-eyed being. They moved closer, but Sam did not need to see him; she knew who it was.

"Kazune," Sam said as she shifted back to her natural form, where she could at least make use of her powers. A blue orb of light floated between her palms and lit the entirety of the cave. The other set of eyes belonged to Nagha, who stepped forth from the shadows. She looked back at the wolf . . . "Maddie?"

"Astute. Though, I no longer underestimate you. You're quite a bit more powerful than I expected," his tone cool and calm in the face of her fiery display. "There's no one left to help you. They're all gone: Rose, your father, the tribe. Don't worry, they're still alive . . . for now. I imagine the sulfur in the other tube will overwhelm them at some point, though. Don't count on my traitorous son to save you either. He's being dealt with."

The pieces of the puzzle fell into place fast: the collapsed section of the lava tube, the missing tribe, Deyo's echoes of pain. Her instincts had been spot on—Maddie had set them up, and perhaps worst of all, Maddie was Ch'iyone.

But Mr. Ezerza had said she was to be the great wolf.

She released a ball of energy toward Kazune and Nagha; they barely needed to move to avoid the misdirected shot. The giant wolf knocked Sam to the floor, tearing at her peacoat. The cave pitched into blackness and she transformed back into an Ijiraq. She could see, but the sharp blades of the wolf's claws sliced through the fur and down her scapula. It burned red hot and she screamed in agony, physical pain like she'd never felt, not even when she nearly died saving Ash and Cinder.

The snarling beast on her back, Sam willed herself to her hindquarters and fell backward as hard as she could into the sharp, jagged lava lining the cave walls. Maddie yelped and let go as Sam let out a cry of her own. Strangely, the warmth of blood pouring from her wounds somehow felt . . . good.

Sam whirled in rage, ready to pierce the wolf with her mangled weave of horns when the entire mountain shook and boiling steam burst from deep within the lava tube, sending the elder Ijiraq tumbling to the ground. A soft red glow formed in the darkness, pulsating like a candle flame. Mount Edziza rumbled again, and more steam released from its depths. The light joined its source—a wave of magma—molten rock sloshing toward her.

Sam turned, running for the portal entrance—a scream silenced: Kazune overcome by the lava.

Sam reached the moonlit entrance and a hoof reached

down for her. "Quick, Dene. Shift and grab my hand." But she hesitated, her people trapped behind the collapsed wall; she couldn't leave them.

A black wind and flash of red rushed by Sam's head— Nagha flew free from the mountain, nearly colliding with Deyo, still begging for Sam's hand.

"They're trapped! I can't leave them," said Sam

Deyo briefly transformed into Puck to join Sam underground. "We don't have time, Dene. We must trust that they'll be safe from the lava flow."

A howl of distress echoed from across the cave. Maddie.

"Dene, no!"

It was too late; Sam shifted, bounding toward the river of fire. She reached the mouth of the left side lava tube and found the young girl battered and bruised but in her usual form, meek and helpless. The lava had slowed as it hit a short uphill section of the cave but was rising quickly. Maddie had barely made it this far, her right foot severely blistered where her paw had briefly come into contact with the lava.

Sam picked Maddie up as the river crested the berm and began flowing down again, her hoof coming inches from the blazing liquid. Deyo was waiting and pushed Maddie from below, birthing her from the cave entrance. Sam was next.

Sam got up to dust herself off and realized her

companion was not behind her. "Deyo! Deyo!" she yelled into the opening. She absorbed a fiery blast of steam, knocking her away from the lava which began pouring from the side of the mountain. Sam planted her face into the warming red silt of the mountainside and screamed, "No!" over and over.

She stopped when a giant hand grabbed her by the ankle and pulled her thirty feet backward across the volcano. She flipped over to see Tall Man standing over her, barely visible but for the glow of the nearby lava which lit his broken face—damage surely doled out by Deyo.

Sam readied a fireball. "No! Please don't!" Maddie begged for the man's life.

"Tell me why! Why should I let him live? Why should I let either of you live after the death and destruction you created!" Sam growled through gritted teeth. "They are all gone! My dad. Your brother. The entire tribe! But you think you deserve life?"

"We all deserve life, and surely you think that too, or you wouldn't have saved me," responded Maddie.

"Call it a moment of weakness, but I've learned my lesson." Sam reared back with a ball of energy—not fire— her eyes flaming sapphires. She wanted them to feel every ounce of her pain electrocuting their bodies, hitting every last nerve in their final moments, to their last breath.

The execution would be stayed. Sam was again grabbed from behind, this time by a pair of large talons that

dragged her skyward several hundred feet, directly over the river of lava. An ear-piercing screech shattered her eardrums as she was falling to a fiery death.

Mere feet from melting, Sam shifted and swooped across the mountainside, climbing swiftly out of danger.

Below, she watched as the raven of death landed on top of Maddie and Tall Man, then shifted: *Nagha!*

The beast began to stamp and stomp at them, his horns running through Tall Man's left bicep and hurtling him down the side of the volcano. Maddie started rolling down the sandy mountain to avoid Nagha's pounding.

Sam hovered above, watching. She could help them if she wanted to, but she was angry, so angry. Voices filled her head: *These are your people, Sam. Save them*, she heard Nana Rose say. *Please, Princess, show compassion, as others have shown for you*, said her mother's voice. Sam continued to watch in contemplation, her feelings betraying her sense of tribe and family. She had to let go of the anger.

She did.

Sam dove straight down at full-speed, wings tucked, and didn't stop until her hooked beak penetrated Nagha's hindquarters, sending them both tumbling hundreds of feet, end over end to the bottom of the mountain, where a tree stopped their momentum far too suddenly.

They writhed in pain. Sam shifted back to human form; her leg broken. She scooted on her behind until she was clear of the monster and rested against a stump.

Nagha shook himself conscious and attempted to stand, but faltered and ended up on all fours, his glorious rack of horns destroyed, scattered across the lower part of the mountain save for three jagged points on his left side and two on his right.

"You just don't know when to stop, do you, little girl?" panted Nagha.

Sam didn't reply. She could barely make sense of what he was saying, ringing ears and vertigo overcoming her senses.

"Hahaha. The mouthy brat has finally been silenced. I'll relish this glory and bask in your life force for eternity." Nagha approached and—still incapable of standing on his hind legs—sat back on his haunches, ready to gore Sam and end the Tahltan Nation once and for all. He lunged and Sam rolled to avoid death.

As she pushed herself up on her hands, she was staring at *paws*—huge paws. Sam had shifted on instinct. She looked back and noticed a tail and could feel her mouth salivating across a full set of canines. She was Ch'iyone!

Nagha shook off his miss and readied himself again. "Look who has a new trick," he said. "Should I be afraid? Ch'iyone is dead. You're a mere impostor."

Sam growled and backed up ever so slightly as the pain of her broken leg accompanied her new form. She knew the power of the great wolf was immense, but she questioned her abilities with the severity of her injuries. She

limped backward and Nagha continued to pursue, matching her step for step, biding his time for the perfect moment to attack.

Behind Nagha, a flash up on the mountain caught Sam's attention. Her keen eyes picked up an army of ants scattering from the side of the volcano. *They're alive! Dad! Deyo!* she called out, not worried who would hear the message.

"They can't help you now." Nagha bounded toward her, horns down, ripping across her left ear as she fell over to avoid the blow. Sam flipped to her feet and quickly grasped Nagha by the nape of the neck with her powerful jaws and bore down. The Ijiraq screamed, but it only made him angry as he began to shake and shake until she finally unclenched and dropped him. He laughed a sinister laugh. "See, not Ch'iyone. Just little Sam, the wolf pup," he continued mocking.

Nagha rose on his hind legs, finally able to stand, towering over her maimed form. Ready to unleash death upon her—the final blow—he reared back as a wooden spear pushed through his stomach. Behind him stood Maddie and Tall Man, his hands holding the other end of the weapon. Nagha spun, throwing the pair to the forest floor, and redirected his rage at the weaker, easier prey.

Maddie and Tall Man saved her. She was ready to destroy them in her anger, but they came back for her, and now they were in danger, once again. Deyo and Yalé were racing down the volcano to help, but there wasn't time.

Sam righted herself, whimpering through the pain of her broken leg, and lunged at Nagha's ankle. She bit down hard—so hard, the crunching of bone echoed through the trees.

Sam—Ch'iyone—ran as fast as she could. She ran through the pain, pulling the Ijiraq with her deep into the forest, away from the others. She didn't stop, and soon the pain gave way to her powerful wiles. Nagha was a rag doll in her mouth.

Sam didn't know where she was going, just that she needed to get the beast as far away from the Tahltan as possible. Then and only then she would figure out how to finish him, though his body bouncing off the passing trees and rocks was undoubtedly satisfying.

Sam ran for hours through the dark at full speed—running on pure adrenaline and never out of breath—until she reached the cliff edge of the Stikine River. She made a hard right to avoid going over the edge but miscalculated—she was falling. They were both falling, done in by a patch of black ice.

Two hundred feet later, they splashed down and were racing down current, before she could shift into a more suitable form, a vortex opened in the waters. The whirlpool lit up from below in purples and greens and blues, twining with a bright white light.

The swirling waters pulled Sam under. She was

falling again, this time into the depths of an inescapable abyss.

Everything went black.

CHAPTER TWENTY-TWO

A hot breeze and the sound of rustling caused Sam to stir. Flat on her back, she attempted to open her eyes, but everything was blurry and the flood of light forced her eyes shut again. Glimpses—shadows and shapes were all she could make out, though she could feel herself . . . moving. Her hazy vision provided only enough information to think she was traveling in an open-ended wooden cart full of hay, its squeaky wheels bumping over a winding dirt path going uphill. Wherever she was, it was not Telegraph Creek, not the Stikine Valley, not even British Columbia.

The cart stuttered over a large pothole in the road. It jarred her, reminding her that her leg was broken—shattered—sending screams of agony echoing through whatever valley they were traveling. *They* . . . it was her final thought as the unbearable pain sent her back into the black.

Sam sat up, shaken from her nightmare: Nagha was bearing down on her with a full, sharpened rack and she had no way to escape. Her powers were gone; she was just ordinary Sam, before she knew of any special abilities residing within her. No fireballs or blue light energy. No shifting between species. No lifesaving or healing.

The suddenness of her movements brought pain, though more of a minor ache now that her leg was splinted and bandaged. She sparked an emerald flame between her thumb and index finger. *Phew, just a dream.*

Her vision was crystal, but the sights she beheld had her believing she was still in dreamland. Sam laid in a smallish, for her, rickety wooden bed. The blankets covering her were made of animal hides, but the pattern and feel of the hides were unlike anything she'd seen: pure white— almost transparent— with lavender spots ringed in an odd shade of green—*neon pea green*—as if there were such a color; the downy texture opposed the hair-like appearance.

"Hello?" Sam called out, scouring the details of the room, wondering where this dream was leading her. The roof was thatched with thousands of twining vines, the walls mostly wood, but interspersed with a grayish plaster which held the shanty together—barely, it seemed.

The small room was hardly big enough for the bed,

but a makeshift table, a log with a simple plank, was covered in baubles. Several handmade stone and wood figurines were arranged in four neat columns, five deep, each on its own square space. *Perhaps a game board?* Each one was different, but she couldn't identify the pieces. One resembled a unicorn but had three horns and a dragon's tail; another looked like a mermaid, with a long, manta ray-like stinger trailing from the center of its fluke. *Strange indeed.*

Then a particular piece caught her eye, and Sam backed away on instinct, finding herself on the dusty, earthen floor on the far side of the bed. Careful of her leg, she pulled herself up and peered across the bed at the table and board. *An Ijiraq?* Though most of the Ijiraq looked nearly identical, this particular piece seemed all too familiar. The likeness was uncanny: *Dene Kazune.*

Sam pulled herself across the hides on her stomach and continued to examine the other figures when another caught her eye, and she couldn't help but reach out and grab it. "Ash," she whispered as she placed the figurine flat in her palm. Warmness welled against her skin where the phoenix met her hand, and slowly, wisps of flames began to jump from the wings and tail feathers of the carving. Sam wasn't scared, but enthralled. For a moment, Ash was with her again. Then, without warning, the statue flashed and disintegrated, and in the blink of an eye, regenerated into its original form. "Whoa," she said with a light chuckle. She didn't know what else to say.

After watching it die and come back to life several times, Sam finally set the phoenix down and wondered what would happen if she touched the others. She grabbed the least ominous of them all, a doe-like creature, a deer, normal as she'd ever seen, but maned like a lion. It stayed motionless . . . then, a waggle of its stubby tail and a shake of its golden mane. Then the animal in her palm shifted, but just the head, resembling a still-golden-maned viper, it reared up on its hind legs. It hissed and spat at Sam, the expelled liquid, just a few droplets, landing on her forearm and burning pits into her skin. Sam jumped from the pain and the statue fell. By the time it hit the bed, it had resumed its original, lifeless form.

Sam grabbed her arm and put an end to the pain and the injury with a healing glow. At least she had that power back, too. Swiftly, she grabbed the piece and placed it back on its spot before it could come back to life and do any more damage. But her curiosity got the best of her . . . She touched the mermaid but did not pick it up. Its eyes blinked a few times and the stinger tail flicked back and forth. Sam removed her touch; she'd learned her lesson.

"Hello? Is anyone there?" she yelled out again, hoping, but fearful of who or what would answer. Still, no answer. Sam snapped her fingers and a ball of crimson energy materialized. She pressed the magic down upon her wrapped and splinted leg. She winced but said nothing, not even a hiss. Scooting to the edge of the bed, without pause she steadied her full weight on the leg. An ear-piercing scream followed and she fell onto her back, breathing hard through the pain.

She laid there until the throbbing subsided, then wiped a solitary tear from her cheek. Her powers were back, but she was still weak—no doubt from the energy she consumed as Ch'iyone and dragging Nagha for miles. She needed to eat.

Sam spied a twisting piece of wood leaning against the foot of the bed. It was smooth and polished, the grain of the wood waving, seemingly alive. A knob sat atop the stick—a tree knot left in place by the craftsman to act as a handle. A cane . . . meant for her. She grabbed the walking stick, and sure enough, the wood grains moved like the ocean tides—a fine piece of ancient, magical art. She touched the waves but felt only the hardness of the wood grains.

Sam cautiously placed the brunt of her weight on the knobby end and pulled herself upright. Still a bit weak on her legs, she fell back on to the bed, the mattress giving under her weight. To her astonishment, the cane was still in its place, standing on end where she had let go, waiting for her return.

She grabbed and pulled at the stick, but it remained solidly in place. This time, she pulled as hard as she could and yanked herself to her feet with a small hop onto her good leg. The cane released and allowed her to move

forward, then stuck again, steadying her next step. Each step, the cane aided her with its magic.

Sam made her way to the narrow doorway and peeked out. The rest of the dwelling looked similar to the bedroom: knickknacks decorated every corner of what she assumed was the main room, a single wooden chair sat adjacent to a large stone hearth which was burning strong and filled the room with a smoky-sweet smell that was somehow familiar. The stuffed head of a frightening creature hung from above.

The unfamiliar animal had four death-black eyes as big as baseballs, two on each side of its head. The skull was oblong, horse-like, but its mouth seemed unusually small given its size, and the animal was completely hairless. No fur, no feathers, no covering of any kind—that, perhaps, more than any of the other features, was the most frightening—even more so than the thorned horns protruding from its rear jawline, twisting up and over the top of the head where they conjoined. Truly the stuff of nightmares—a lucid one Sam was convinced she was still having.

An entryway sat opposite the fireplace and was framed by two open windows. A warm breeze pushed in, and she thought it curious to have a fire burning on such a temperate day. Sam turned her shoulders sideways to get through the doorway and limped to the center of the room, still aided by the magic cane and continuing to take in the eclectic decor. A wetness to the air clashed with the dryness of the fire's heat, sending an odd chill through her body.

"Hello?" she said again, and again with no answer. She was convinced she was alone, at least for the moment, and it gave her some respite that whoever brought her here wouldn't have tended to her injuries if they were all that bad.

Sam walked to the nearest window in search of clues of her whereabouts. "I'm not in Kansas anymore, Toto." She'd seen The Wizard of Oz at least a dozen times; it was her mom's favorite movie.

The landscape that greeted her was unlike anything; to say it was dreamlike was an understatement. The skies were not blue, but lavender—even lighter—casting a hue across the landscape. Above, a large tangerine sun dominated a third of the sky, its heat far less proportional and looking as though it would collide with whatever planet she was on. Sam stuck her arm out of the window to feel it on her skin. "It's perfect," she said.

The yard surrounding the house was filled with dozens of foreign flowers of differing types, and in the center of the fenced property sat a mammoth tree at least fifty feet in diameter at the base and twisting five hundred feet high. Its branches were thin for its size but full of leaves that rustled in the breeze. When the wind stopped, the leaves continued, as though . . . "It's alive." Sam was mesmerized as the leaves didn't just dance in place, sans wind; they moved back and forth along the branches,

272

switching places with each other and reattaching.

When the winds picked back up, a few of the leaves, which had yet to reattach floated toward the ground, but before they hit the flawless, emerald grass, they sprouted tiny feathers along their ridges and flitted back to the safety of the branches. "What is this place?"

"Ah, I see you've discovered the Tree of Iniquity," said a deep yet soft voice from behind her. Sam whirled with a fireball in hand. "But don't let its beauty fool you; it's quite the crafty devil, hence its name. Please, come sit and rest . . . put down your defenses," he said, turning his back to Sam and disappearing into the room opposite the bedroom.

The man was tiny, just over half of Sam's five-foot, five-inch frame. His hair was mid-back length and pure white, save for two jet black streaks which ran down either side of his head—his beard matched the stripes.

"Who are you? Where am I?" Sam called to him.

When he returned, he said, "Please, sit, sit." He had a steaming bowl of unknown liquid balanced in his Lilliputian fingers, but Sam remained frozen, not letting the fireball dissipate. "You need to rest and eat, please; I don't want to ask again." It seemed like a mild threat, but Sam didn't want to find out.

She complied and moved gently across the room until she was almost directly under the taxidermized monster, her eyes fixed inches from its grotesque visage.

"Never mind that. Just a decoration. It's not even a

real. You'd know if it were. Even without its body, it's still a vile creature capable of deathly things. Nope, just a decoration from Kartan's Bazaar. Kartan himself made it 'specially for me, in honor of my youth, when I escaped one, just barely. Not many have lived to tell of their encounter with a Drox. Thankfully its Senasac rider had dismounted while hunting its victim—an encounter with the Senasac is inescapable. Sit, sit."

Sam was overwhelmed by the man's nonstop oration and the apparent perilous world in which she found herself. Devilish trees, unkillable monsters, venomous figurines . . . "Where am I?" Sam asked again, convinced she was dreaming. Maybe the dream was trying to tell her something about what happened after falling into the Stikine River—though this felt a little too real.

"There'll be plenty of time for questions and answers later." Sam was forced into the seat. The man waved a hand toward her, and she could feel a force press against her. Though gentle, it was enough that she involuntarily found herself where he'd asked her to be.

"Good, now eat. You need to regain your strength. This will help your leg . . . and your magic." He handed Sam the piping hot bowl, which she accepted with shaking hands. "Good, good, there you are. Go ahead, eat."

Sam lifted the bowl to her mouth. Afraid of burning her lips, she carefully tipped the contents toward her partially open mouth. It smelled peppery, not unpleasant,

almost like a stew, though it didn't appear to be anything but broth. The man stood back, mimicking her motion with the bowl. She wasn't sure if she was complying with his wishes or he was force-feeding her with whatever magic he used to seat her in the chair.

Her lips touched the overly warm bowl, and as the liquid poured in and down her throat, Sam coughed hard. The soup was ice cold, and she pulled back from the dish and grabbed her head. Brain freeze. Perhaps it would've been tolerable if the dish tasted like ice cream or some other sweet, icy treat, but this healing potion was anything but. It was salty and bitter and tasted of rotten lamb. Sam had no idea how she could possibly know that particular flavor, but it's what she surmised nonetheless, and the taste festered in her mouth.

"Oh, oops, I'm sorry," said the man. "I suppose I should have let you know about that. Not all is as it seems here. Not like in your world. Hot is cold; cold is hot. There's a surprise at every turn. Please, though, finish, or you'll be slow to heal, and your powers are needed."

Sam's frozen headache warmed, and she slammed the bowl and its remaining contents at the man's feet. Her eyes flashed crystal blue. "This is the last time I will ask . . . Who are you, and where am I?"

The old man simply smiled and said, "My name is Yadaray. Welcome to Karavan."

GLOSSARY

Behgehyalé	Butterfly
Ch'iyone	Wolf
Dene	Person (shortened from Dene Ti'e meaning "Boss" and used for the word "Chief")
Deyo	Moose, Bull
Hodzih	Caribou
Inuksuk	Manmade rock formations or cairns used by indigenous peoples of Canada and Alaska
Kazune	Otter
Nagha	Wolverine
Tsesk'iye	Raven, crow

For more information about the Talhtan language, visit:

www.tahltanlanguage.com
www.Tahltan.org/language
www.firstvoices.com

Joel Thomas Feldman is a husband, father, military veteran, engineer, and author. With a bachelor's degree in TV/Film, and master's in Strategic Intelligence, Joel has spent his career working in and around the U.S. Air Force. Joel lives in Southern California with his wife, Michaela, and their two children, Jack and Thais.

Learn more about the author at:

Joelthomasfeldman.com
Instagram.com/joelthomasfeldman

Made in the USA
Middletown, DE
06 March 2022

62090611R00168